INFINITY

(A VÉGTELEN)

Kiára Árgenta

OPENING CHAPTER

First Printing, 2014

ISBN 10: 1-904958-37-0

ISBN 13: 9781904958376

published by

Opening Chapter
Cardiff, Wales

www.openingchapter.com

I write this for you.
Always.
K

JEGES POKOL

Temető

I'm crying in the cemetery
Wearing my ivory wedding dress
Antique frosted icing
Drips over the prostrate stone

It seems like the end of the world
As I trace the outline of his name
With polished black fingernails
Born 1943
Died 1990
I press my face into the tomb
In the chill November still
And howl

Some people carrying flowers
to another lost soul
look over in sympathy

But I didn't know him

I have always been a sad girl and opted for tragedy.
Happy endings are just not in my lexicon. I chose to
study languages because I like the way they carve
their shapes; unique and distinct with no need for
analysis. To me languages have personalities like the
glittering stars in *The Great Gatsby*'s parties all
clamouring for attention. Finnish sounds like the
formation of ice crystals whereas Italian sounds like
musical mozzarella cheese; stretchy and beautiful.
There are happier souls out there for sure. I got a

circular letter from my cousin last Christmas. Every month of the year was listed such as *'May started out as a happy month with all well with us here in the village. I am fortunate that I can stay at home and look after our three darling children. I am truly blessed.'*

Oh, cousin Giovanna, my heart truly does bleed for you. Not.

I typed a slightly changed up version such as *'my husband has been taking us to a lot of swingers' parties recently and I don't know what to do. Mum is shocked but Dad said that he has been to a few in his time'* and in the middle of a fairytale cupcake month I would put. *'But Marcus came home with the clap for the second time this year after his week in America for a conference'* and then mailed it back to her.

I hope she thinks twice next Christmas and keeps her saccharine-drenched world to herself.

Well the good news is that I am not lying around in cemeteries any longer but fast forward some fifteen years and nothing has really changed; I am lying in the snow in Eastern Europe, except the world is turning faster and faster on its axis these days, or maybe it is just me spinning faster and faster. Cousin Giovanna's life is gilded with pink frosted icing and fairies. Mine is full of swords and strife and strange sounding languages with sharp accents. Even my languages are spiky such as Hungarian with its unusual alphabet and bristling accents. Hungarian is an outsider like me; it doesn't fit into Europe. It is the sharp unnatural shape in the smooth rounded jigsaw of languages.

That is okay with me; this is how I choose to live, or more like how life has chosen me to live it.

I am lying on my back in Lithuania in a blizzard. The snow is swirling into my face and the wind is like a razor. This fake fur is useless and I have slipped in my sky-high stiletto shoes. Why am I dressed like this in the Baltics in Spring which is still Winter and dragging my suitcase to the overpriced hostel I booked? I must be mad. My brain will not stop churning. The wheels of my suitcase are stuck in a snowdrift. I am sick; I am bipolar and this is frozen Hell. It's Easter and I'm suffering like Christ. Maybe I should be dragging a crucifix; it would be more fitting.

The sky as I look up from where I have fallen is an unforgiving white and I have the feeling I have reached the end of the line. Why do I always end up in the worst places on a national holiday? I have a magnet in my heart for hunting down bad experiences. Everything in the frozen wasteland which is masquerading as Vilnius is shut apart from some overpriced restaurants serving soup in hollowed out bread bowls. I spend 3 days in bed as it's the only way to get warm. Latvia and Lithuania still have the old Soviet style heating in many buildings where it snaps on 1st November and turns off 1st April and it never gets warm enough.

I cry all the way from Vilnius to Riga through the snowstorm, the same cutting wind, the same miserable run-down bus station and the same depression and the same question; what in Hell's name am I doing here? Everyone else looks depressed as can be so I am in good company at least. I can cry freely, without shame and an old lady takes my arm and says in Russian that this is a very bad winter, this weather is gloomy beyond belief, and helps me on to the coach. *Hell has frozen over officially,* she says.

I can no longer use God's name as I would sit for an

hour before the crucifix in cathedrals across Europe and after many years I denounced God and only dealt in black magic. At the border with Latvia, I can see nothing as we are in a white-out but a border guard stops our bus from his wooden hut and climbs on, looks at everyone and their passports and stops at me. He looks at me and at my passport and shakes it, as if it is fake. He is suspicious. I am going from one white wilderness to another and he thinks I am travelling on a fake passport.

I should have learned something when I studied Russian at Swansea University and spent a miserable paper-pushing year at university in Latvia and working part-time at a local Russian language newspaper. I was depressed all the time in the cold and grey and when the first rays of warmth punctured the Baltic gloom it was well into June. I should have learned that my body needs heat and sun and light and back then I was padded with enough flesh to make me normal weight. Now I am skeletal due to all the stress.

Chiara Argenta: I am Kiára Árgenta now as when I first moved to Hungary no one could pronounce my name and I changed it by deed poll. The soft letter 'g' in my surname is trouble too, but I can't change it to a Hungarian-friendly equivalent. Half-Welsh, quarter-Sicilian, quarter-Icelandic and one hundred percent bipolar. You could divide me up like a cake but those ingredients do not mix. My supermodel Icelandic grandmother spent her whole life fighting with my Sicilian grandfather. Why do you think they put those countries so far apart? I inherited her appearance, her bone structure but with a darker twist and a Sicilian temperament.

I look Hungarian and when people find out I'm not,

they search for answers. But are your parents Hungarian? Why are you here? It's a mystery to them why I am in this landlocked place with its impossible language that I have to study for hours a day to make any kind of progress.

Hungary like me has its own bipolarity; melting hot summers and miserable sometimes subzero winters. In the summer the light gives the buildings a rose-tinted glow. It's beautiful and the sunshine is endless, then round about 10th October something happens. The weather gets sick; it slides from cool sunny days into endless grey gloom. The buildings are grey, the people are grey, a violinist plays the lamenting '*Gloomy Sunday*' otherwise known as the Hungarian suicide song round the grey cold castle in Budapest.

I left the United Kingdom as it no longer felt like my country. I am a European nomad gathering a string of lovers, languages and pain. I need the pain to feel alive. To sit in Wales in the job I was doing for the television station would be like nailing down my coffin forty years too soon. I was fired from my job due to posing naked for an Italian fashion magazine. I was in Rome on holiday and offered the work and thought no one would find out. They were beautiful arty shots, like *La Dolce Vita* style, my favourite film, and anyway, nothing is really visible. It went unnoticed for a couple of years until some back-stabber or other, who knows as there were so many back-stabbers, found out. I was called into the director's office and fired.

After that there was no good reason to stay UK based. I headed to Spain. Until then I'd been a plain old depressive and that's when, under the burning Canarian sun, the mania which was already threatening to take me over each Summer, started to burst through with a murderous intensity.

ÉGÉS ŐRÜLTSÉG

I am staring at the flag of Uruguay on the wall. It shimmers due to all the Jägermeister and Mojitos and Red Bull which has led to this blackout where I lost some hours. It's 4am as I am staring at my wrist and my heart is pounding like it will explode through my chest and break the silence. I wonder who I am and how I ended up in South America. There's a young man asleep next to me. I manage to gather myself to get up, put some fresh contact lenses in and find my bag. I leave with my shoes in my hands so I can get away quietly, only the street is dark and I have no sense of direction. I ask a man coming towards me the way to the port. I have remembered I'm in Gran Canaria but I have no idea how to get home. My heart is in such overdrive I don't know how I will survive this.

He asks me in Spanish *don't I know him?*
Why would I? I never saw him before in my life.

He tells me that I ran out of his apartment just now. This could be funny but it's not, I am beyond this kind of behaviour. Blacking out and not knowing where I am. I'm 31 not 16. I was drinking to forget István's lookalike I had a disastrous fling with in Gran Canaria to try to forget István and Hungary but this is not working, clearly. Everything is spinning in circles and I keep ending up running into what I am running away from. I am 4000 km from the man I love and all I can think of is István. I am unravelling in paradise where the sun shines 363 days of the year and the sunsets and moon rises are the most beautiful I have ever seen. Everyone here is running away from something or someone; leaving their jobs, their lives scattered across Europe and drinking in the sun to forget.

I make it back to the house I am staying in and swallow a load of klonopin to get me to sleep and stop me crying. It is 5am and I am a wreck. I curl up next to István's photo and put Lana Del Rey on a loop on my music player. The cat never approaches me normally, but this night or morning or whatever Hell or half-light it is in my head she knows I need comfort. She leaps on to my pillow, wraps herself around me in consolation and settles at the foot of my bed. She waits until I sleep before she closes her eyes, this feline guardian of dreams. In the morning she doesn't leave until I get up.

An old hobo man is living on the edge of the cliff near to where I am staying. It is like something out of a Fellini film. His bed is virtually hanging over the cliff edge and there is a mirror wedged into the rock face and some old furniture. It never rains so he doesn't have to worry. I go to visit him with a friend and he gestures to sit down. The bed and chairs are horribly stained. Would we like a drink of wine?

Yes, but if we drink one here who knows what infection we'll pick up.

We decline politely saying we are not thirsty.

One morning I hear helicopters and we find out he stumbled over the cliff face in the night and drowned in the sea. Surreal in life, surreal in death, this displaced man, Mikhail from Ukraine who said he never felt at home anywhere chose to live on a rock face far from everyone he knew. He ended up a citizen of nowhere, buried anonymously. This made me feel very sad. I am afraid I will end up like him, a drifter, a nobody who belongs nowhere and no one will care. This is a wake up call for me. I have to stop drifting.

I am dancing on tables every night but I'm not being paid. I'm just drinking and popping pills and getting high from the sunshine. I have to get off this rock otherwise I will die. I have to get back to István and Hungary. I leave as the cruel Calima moves in shrouding the air in the Canary Islands in sand which shows up on satellite pictures and on the lungs of all the asthmatics.

AJÁNDÉKOK

In our happy time together
You gave me

One diamond necklace
A thousand red roses
A trip to the Ice Hotel in Kiruna
A silver sports car
A lifetime of promises

Plenty of headaches

A collapsed windpipe
Two concussions
Third degree burns
Four broken ribs
Five death threats

A few million insults and enough jaw damage
to outlive the lifetime of promises

It is the days pre-István and pre-Hungary and I am
shivering not with cold but fear. The man I live with
in Valencia has just come back into our apartment
threatening to kill me. He has already permanently
damaged my jaw but I am waiting just a bit longer to
have sufficient funds to run. I've been in Spain for two
years and we have lived in endless apartments in
Eivissa, Menorca, Mallorca, Lanzarote and Valencia
but the relationship was dead after one year pretty
much. All this moving around is a promise to save us.
It'll be better in Eivissa, no it'll be better in
Lanzarote. I'll write better here, there, anywhere. He

says the same thing about his work. This bar will work, I know it will. Like me he once worked in television and now he has grand ideas about how to make money. They all fail disastrously so he plays *Euromillions* thinking he will make a big scoop, spending more and more on lottery tickets each week. I tell him how pointless this is when he wins ten or twenty euros at times and then goes and buys even more tickets with the money. The playing is entirely self-reflexive.

Our latest Salvador Dali themed bar has left him way out of pocket. I have a Latvian bank account he doesn't know about otherwise I wouldn't be able to hide my money. I have told him I am leaving. I should have left the night he damaged my jaw, hitting me over the kitchen counter into a load of wine glasses. My teeth looked fine so I ignored it for some time, thinking it was okay. It was far from okay. He bandaged my arm and told me he loved me. I ignored the pain in my jawbone.

Tonight, he has been out with one of his stupid macho friends. By the time he comes home and I am asleep, he is whipped up into a frenzy of hate; hate of me and all women; we are all the same to him. He never thinks any of this is his fault. He is drunk and yelling the worst insults, while I am sober in my nightdress unable to reach my cell phone to call the Guardia for help. He is threatening to kill me. I look at the floor and curl into a ball hoping that he will just wear himself out and I will get out of here alive. None of the neighbours call the police either as we live in a Spanish apartment block and the sound of men screaming at their wives or beating their girlfriends is endemic in Spain. He is spitting and pacing up and down the room and in the end he runs out and locks me in. It is a hot June night, 2am and I have told him calmly some days ago that I am leaving him. He is not taking it too well. He hasn't eaten all week.

When I hear him lock the door and run out, I drag my hidden suitcase out of the wardrobe and get dressed. The rest of the clothes I will just leave. We live on the second floor but I am agile. I lower my suitcase as far as I can over the balcony and drop it onto a load of towels. I follow it but I don't need to drop. It's easy to climb onto the balcony downstairs and then I land like a cat on the grass below. I head away from the seafront as I know that's where he was headed. He was shouting about going to drown himself in the Med as he ran out. I head as far into the city as I can and pick up a cab on the way. I take a train to Madrid. All I can think of is the one possession I left behind that was of any value to me; a rubber Salvador Dali clock. It's still in the bar he owns. I got it from an exhibition I visited with my mother and it is straight out of the painting *The Persistence of Memory*. It is molten and floppy and I could drape it over an armchair. I forgot to pack the goddamn clock. I loved that clock. I obsess about the clock all the way to Madrid probably to stop me thinking about how my life has gone so horribly pear-shaped. Distorted and twisted like my beloved clock, time stretching out into unnatural proportions without warning, then suddenly snapping back and speeding up.

I don't want to return to Wales so I make some calls to people I know while I stay in a hostel in Madrid. Someone I met last year in Lanzarote invites me to stay in her Austrian cottage. It sounds like a good plan. I have never been to Austria before. Maybe I can recuperate.

Like Hell. I get sick from the plane which is rammed full to Bratislava, and then I get a train to Vienna and I know the chest infection is well on its way as I get off in the middle of nowhere in the Rax Alps. Tessa meets me at the train station and says she's sorry but she has no car and we just missed the bus but no problem, there's another one in 2 hours.

The first thing I notice is her awful shoes and her terrible mismatch of clothing. She looks like a lesbian traffic warden on her day off. I tell myself not to be so critical, a hangover from growing up in Paris and constantly striving to have style. The next thing I notice in the silence of the empty station is that Tessa talks and talks and then some more. In fact Tessa will talk non-stop for fifteen hours a day for the next godawful two weeks. Still, I try to be optimistic; the bus arrives, the sun is shining and I have escaped my hell of domestic abuse. I have no phone as I didn't want a crazed ex-boyfriend texting, calling and leaving endless messages so I just chucked it in a bin as I was entering the train station in Valencia.

As we walk up the lane from the bus stop to Tessa's house, I see chocolate box pretty alpine cottages with immaculate gardens, some with flowers and silver baubles and beautifully decorated. I hope hers is as nice. A broken down tiny white building sits sullenly at the end.

"Here we are," sings Tessa. *No shit.*

I walk in and the smell of cat food and stale air hits me first. I see flies buzzing round dirty plates, the floor in the kitchen is filthy and worst of all there is a toilet next to the fridge. *A toilet next to the fridge. This is unbelievable.* It will get worse when Tessa cooks and places the dinner plates on the lid to dish up but I don't know this yet.

"Where's the bathroom?" I ask, already knowing the answer.

"Oh, I don't have one but you can have a wash in this big bucket here and wash your hands in the sink and look, here's the living room."

It is tiny and stuffed with a sofa-bed and a table and a couple of armchairs which look like they should have died 200 years ago together with the dirtiest lace curtains in the world. To reach her bedroom, Tessa has to go outside and climb up a rickety ladder and in through the window.

I should just run now before this chest infection takes its grip.

But I don't.

And the weather turns into autumn for the next two weeks. It rains in that miserable Welsh damp way where the slanting drops get into your face and your bones. There is no TV, no internet, one bus every 20 years or so and the nearest village is 2 hours' walk away. I am sick and cough and cough as Tessa talks and talks. Each night on my broken spring sofa-bed I curse my bad decisions as I listen to the rain and each morning I put my feet straight on to the dead mice the cats leave in my shoes.

When I leave this Hellhole Tessa shouts I have let her down, let the cats down and rejected her hospitality. Didn't I know she bought muesli for me? Moreover, I have broken an agreement by leaving 2 days early.

Agreement? Excuse me but when did this house visit become legally binding?

She shouts as I make my way down the road to wait for the bus. The cheapest thing I can do is get a train to Vienna, then a bus to Prague. Prague is supposed to be beautiful.

I am so stressed I spend the whole five days in Prague wandering around in the rain feeling that these famous cities are always overpriced and overrated and sitting in the hostel bar drinking flaming absinthes through the sugar slotted spoon and staring at the strange hexagonal coins which make up the Czech currency. I then fall out of bed at 4am with the worst hangover of my life and decide I have to go to Budapest by train. I can't explain why I am doing this. It is part of my manic condition which bites harder in the summer, this wild impulsiveness. My body reacts to light and has to do things. Of course I don't have to get the 5am train to the Hungarian capital that day. The world won't end; I can wait longer or never. I have no reason to go other than the driving force which propels me through so many countries in search of some mythical honey pot at the end of the rainbow.

And that's where the real story begins. The insulting emails from the ex-boyfriend carry on for some months as he has hacked into my account and read every email I have ever sent. I ignore them all and it goes quiet. He has no idea where I am in the world.

Diet tip of the year; get your jaw whacked out of line by your violent boyfriend. Do nothing for eight months and then when you finally go to the oral-maxillal facial surgeon, he tells you it is irreparably damaged and then you can't eat much. Soup, soft fruit, cheese and yoghurt. Forget having your jaws wired. This is Kiára's solution. Except I don't and didn't need to diet anyway. However, despite my dress size and the weighing scales telling me I am underweight, despite the modelling shots where I look nice, I suffer from body dysmorphia my entire life. It sometimes is in remission, but other times I can hardly bear to look in the mirror. It is worse when life isn't going well and the same voices come back to haunt me, these ghostly echoes of childhood. Then the razors and the cigarette lighters come out and I sit on the bathroom floor and begin my lifelong ritual. Some people use alcohol to numb the pain, I use the burn and the pain to numb the screaming in my head. Alcohol is only a depressant. After a self-harming ritual, I feel calmer, more relaxed and less frenzied but I have to keep buying lot of bandages and making excuses.

MAGYAR LÁNY

I first came to Hungary as I was curious and immediately felt at home in an inexplicable way, as if I had found my long-lost tribe. I learn the Hellishly complex language and use it as much as I can, refusing to associate with any ex-pats. I am downright hostile when any British men try to talk to me. I associate them with the old world, the world where I felt oppressed and depressed and I don't intend to spend my days in a European country speaking English. It is the same reason I wear my high heels every day. I could be dead tomorrow so I have to live for today.

The Hungarian sadness which resonates so perfectly through all the versions of the hauntingly beautiful tune of *Gloomy Sunday* I have heard seems to find a place in my heart. If ever a nation was designed for me then this would be it. I have also always hated Sundays. They have a special sadness of their own which even after everything began to open; shops, bars, restaurants, still permeates everything. Sunday is sad in my mind forever more. I am too depressive even for the Hungarians at times, especially the younger generation. They do not understand me.

I find out that this would be a good place to have my jaw fixed, Hungarian dentistry being the top of the world and that's when I am drawn to István. It is fate from start to finish, not that it ever finishes. We are bonded together through eternity. Not that I know that at this moment as I am lying in his surgery and István is busy fixing my jaw with his gentle rubbery fingers and breaking my heart with his brutish sadistic behaviour. The jaw injury is a legacy of the man I left behind in Spain. Well I still have the diamonds. If things get really tough, I can sell those. István who seemed so handsome and charming when I first arrived in this country is controlling, rabidly jealous and at times completely cruel. I console myself that he is physically not capable of violence although for someone who told me he didn't like arguments he enjoys starting them. He glares with such hatred when I look nice as if I am going to pick up every young man in sight. The colour red is his favourite and yet it fills him so full of burning anger so I try to avoid wearing it.

I hadn't spent long in Budapest after I first arrived in Hungary, instead choosing to travel south to the Mediterranean style city of Pécs. It was too hot, too noisy, too overwhelming in the capital and I needed somewhere I didn't feel so frenzied. I wanted to see the real Hungary. I needed a calmer place to quell the voices in my head and escape the pollution and the buildings blasting out hot summer air. I am not used to this heat with no ocean, no sea breezes and find it very oppressive. I feel unable to breathe.

When I first met István I had stumbled on his dental surgery by accident while I was looking around Pécs with its golden and pink buildings and pretty piazzas and fountains. I had a lifelong morbid fear of the dentist but the cool green entrance seemed to invite me to go in to escape the blistering heat outside. I made up my mind I had to get rid of this dentophobia and I had to see to my jaw. It was getting harder to chew and there seemed to be a loose marble on one side of my jawbone which didn't seem right.

The receptionist smiled and said if I'd like to wait a while, their most experienced dentist who also worked at the hospital as an oral-maxillal facial surgeon, would see me for an assessment. Enter István with his dark eyes lighting up to see me sitting there. He looked Italian to me and I wondered if he had some Mediterranean blood like me. He struck me as too handsome and arrogant in his black Gucci suit. *I bet he knows he is gorgeous,* I thought. *I bet he chases every good looking woman around. I bet he dates women and breaks their hearts and moves on to his next.* I didn't like him, the way he told me I was a very beautiful girl and *did I have a boyfriend?*

See what I mean? *I am not going to be his next roadkill.*

Excuse me, mister but what has that got to do with my teeth?

I bet you ask all the pretty girls that, I said sarcastically.

He looked a bit crumpled by this remark.

No, I don't have a boyfriend. He wrecked my jaw, I tell him. *I just left him in Spain.*

He is cheered up even more by this but *so sorry for my poorly jaw, so I am here all alone then?*

He moves closer and probes gently with his hands each side of my face. I look into his eyes and feel like I am drowning. The feeling is so intense I have to shut my eyes as I feel he is looking right into my soul, as though I have met him somewhere before in another life. He stares into my eyes not my mouth so I have to close my eyes. I let him do his work and the way he touches my face, I feel as though he is working on a sculpture, moulding its soft texture into the shape he wants but so gently and lovingly. I am his clay; malleable and pliable and he can do what he wants. This is a physical manifestation of this thought which will become more real as I am eventually over two years moulded into the woman he wants but I don't know this yet either. He is a magician of manipulation. I just think he is a handsome highly-skilled dentist and surgeon so far; a little bit strange, but I put this down to the linguistic and cultural differences. After all I haven't met a Hungarian man before and surely some comments must get lost in translation.

I was sitting there holding my book of the month; *Csingilling* or Tinkerbell in Hungarian. It's the book of the month as the language is so difficult it takes me that long to read it. It's for five-year olds. István is talking to me now as he eyes my book. This must forever brand me as a child in his eyes, although at 40 he only has ten years on me although I feel like it's about 20.

"And we must schedule in all these appointments for various cosmetic and cleaning treatments, you lovely, lovely girl. Don't you worry about no one now, I will care for your jaw. It is damaged badly, but you don't have to worry about nothing. István the king of Hungary will be your saviour," he says looking at me with those dark depthless eyes.

I like to hear him speak English in his gentle Hungarian-American accent. His use of double negatives in his speech makes me smile. I find it sweet as it contrasts with his arrogant front.

Hell, I'm 30. I leave feeling about ten years old. The reference to István, the first king of Hungary is lost on me at this point as I know very little about Hungarian history before the 1956 uprising.

I don't realise he is only half joking when he refers to himself as the first king of Hungary. Such are his delusions of grandeur he believes he is a reincarnation of the original István. I don't realise part of the reason he is not married is because he is waiting for his Gizella and no one has lived up to his expectations so far. He is also searching for his mythical honey pot at the end of the rainbow.

I went home still afraid of the dental surgery and there was a violent thunderstorm that June evening. The sky was an uncanny pink and forks of lightning shot through the clouds but it did nothing to rid the city of relentless heat. The thunder cracked overhead, moved around in a circle for hours and hours, splitting my dreams into jagged savage pieces. Through my sleep István snaked his way in and I had a disturbing dream that he was a headless horseman and I was kissing him while his head was tucked under one arm. However it changed my opinion; he really was good-looking with his thick black corkscrew curls, lovely creamy skin and dark eyes with those endless black lashes and three days later I was looking forward to seeing him again. He seemed nicer now he was in his dental whites having shed his designer black suit; less arrogant and softer. He was so skilled when he injected my gums I didn't know whether it was the epinephrine in the local anaesthetic or him making my heart race as he bent over me and his soft hair brushed my face and made me shiver.

I am high on a mix of valium and the anaesthetic and I hear myself asking *is he married?*

Why wouldn't he be? I am so off my face I reach out of the dental chair and wrap a jet-black corkscrew curl of his hair round my fingers and it is silky soft, not rough like I imagined. I pull gently and it springs back into place.

He smiles at me adoringly showing his perfect teeth. Only sweetness and no sign of the cobra within.

"Sorry," I tell him.

"No, it is okay" he smiles. "I have never been married." He stares at me way too long with those lovely eyes of his, like he can't quite figure out if I am real.

An angel dropped from Heaven into his dental surgery.

There must be something wrong with him, I think. Someone that good-looking would not be unmarried, work-obsessed or not. I have to look away from the intensity of his gaze. It is really unnerving despite my drugged up state.

I do not know that right now he is thinking he has found his Queen. He has found his lady at last and he can't believe it. I only find all this out after a long, long time after overhearing one of his nightmares. As he is staring at me there, I don't know what is going on. I just think he is very strange and way too intense. Maybe, just maybe he would accept me and my strange behaviour then. Maybe he won't tell me I am crazy like all the other guys.

But he tells me with sadness, *I am sorry, my lady but your jaw is permanently damaged. We can care for it but it is going to be nearly impossible to cure.* He looks at his hands stretching the latex gloves out of shape.

I will do what I can, he says. He points out the damage on a panoramic x-ray, which magnifies the ghost grey jawbone with its damaged ball and socket joint; horribly loose on one side and locked on the other. I am ashamed he knows this information I haven't even told any relatives. I feel he will judge me as a victim. Someone who was smacked by her ex-partner and has only just left him. I feel guilty as Hell, as though I should have left sooner.

I feel as though it was my fault.

He says he can do an operation at the hospital and it will be a minor scar, very small but it is not a problem solver. It will help but it won't cure me. He will have to take care of it for a long, long time.

By the time I realise the true extent of István's character I am hooked. He has suggested only the second time I go there that maybe I would like to eat some nice soft food with him one night? *Something jaw-friendly? He eats out all the time alone and knows the best places.*

He stresses this word **alone.** He is cautious when he asks, as if I am likely to laugh and say no. He is unsure of himself around me.

Why would someone as handsome as him eat alone all the time? Has he some social problem? He is beautiful, charming and successful. Why is he alone? Why is he eating in expensive restaurants without anyone to join him, even friends? Is there something deeply wrong with him? Does he eat like a pig in a trough?

I laugh at this thought.

"What are you laughing at?" he asks. "Be careful not to stretch that jaw."

Well he has a whole truckload of problems but by the time I realise it is way too late to get out. But then who am I to judge as I know, I really know what it is like to be truly fucked up and I can accept it in others. So long as no one is hitting me or hurting me, I will accept their flaws.

When I am scheduled in for jaw surgery at the hospital, he is there as the anaesthetist puts me under with the needle. I feel István's hands stroking my hair and my eyes snap shut like a doll.

As I come round after the anaesthetic those same delicate hands are stroking my hair again.

"Don't try to speak," he whispers. I look into the dark fathomless eyes and claw at my oxygen mask. He tells me to leave it on longer, stay relaxed. The operation was fast, he thinks it will help but it is not a miracle cure. I am going to have to be under his care for a long time. He stresses this word 'long' and it sounds like infinity. There is a flicker of possession in his speech and the way he touches me, like I am his new toy. He has found me broken and now I am being mended by him; I am his. It is only fleeting as I see this emotion in his eyes, like I might see a ghost slide past in a glimmer of light and wonder if I imagined it.

After my operation, he has insisted he supervise my eating of soup and liquid food to ensure my jaw heals a bit before it is put to work. I am left with a tiny scar. I touch it in the mirror. He has branded me as his. It could just as well be a letter 'I' but I think maybe I imagine this.

He has taken me out to lovely restaurants, hung on my every word as if I am the most beautiful woman in existence. He is impressed by my command of languages, the fact that I was a television presenter and the fact I made my way to Hungary and have managed to settle in this alien land alone, unassisted. He is flowing through my veins like junk and I need that fix whether good or bad. And usually it is bad. We have already strayed away from the safety of sweetness and into the vortex of extreme obsession.

He tells me *he has been waiting a lifetime for me. I am his Queen and he is King of Hungary, a reincarnation of István from the year 1000.*

That is nice, I think. *It makes a change for a man to say such dramatic things.*

And he doesn't eat like a pig in a trough as I feared but with such surgical precision and a touch of obsessive compulsive disorder. He measures his plate into exact mouthfuls. He carves up a steak one night as though he is performing heart surgery and extracts a perfect star shape, holding it up to the light in wonder. As he looks at it, he almost forgets I am there. Yes, together with his King István fantasy I have found a strange man.

I do not realise he is deadly serious about this István a Király. He is a reincarnation of the King, he doesn't doubt this. I find this out when he sleeps, some months later and he is shouting every night. With him there will be no peaceful nights. His nightmares and terrors will be so intense, his sleepwalking so disturbing that I will have to sleep with the light on, losing my sleep so I can care for him night after nightmare-filled night.

I get addicted to going to the surgery, switching from dentophobic to dentophiliac overnight thanks to this gorgeous Hungarian and his delicate hands. I have my jaw treated weekly and when the operative stress has worn off, I have my teeth bleached and then rows of sapphire braces on my teeth fitted. One thing I can't figure out with him aside from him never having married at his age which is unusual in Hungary, is his reluctance to get into bed. I wonder if he doesn't find me pretty enough as I am not used to this but some Hungarian women assure me this is a very good sign, it means he is really serious about me and it is part of the old-fashioned dating ritual. He will only kiss or hold my hand, stroke my face as if he is afraid of me and my body. It takes me so long to get to see his apartment I worry he is hiding a secret wife and family somewhere.

And we do just that, we see it. We go there, he shows it to me as if he is an estate agent and we have a coffee. I see absolutely no feminine influence in any of the three bedrooms or anywhere in the bathroom. This is definitely an apartment for one lonely man or someone who hates women. I could make the first move but it has gone on too long for that. I am waiting for him to leap on me.

I don't realise that once I will get into his bed, I will never be able to get out of it; he is as addicted to my body as if it were crystal meth, hence his reluctance to put me in it in the first place. And with this comes the loving the drug and hating it, the resisting the fix, swearing off it and then needing it with every fibre of his body and soul. I don't realise he has the same addictive personality as me; our brains are wired in very similar ways.

Summer slides into autumn and I am teaching some journalism classes at the university and writing articles for Russian newspapers online. I am staying in a beautiful apartment off Széchenyi Tér for a fraction of the price I would pay in Spain but it is hard. I can't sleep. I am depressed. I always slide into depression when the first leaf falls. István doesn't call when he says he will, he gets so wrapped up in his teeth and work that he will switch his phone off and go to sleep. It makes me demented. I end up having to go into his workplace to remind him I exist and his face always lights up in delight and however mad I was with him, I just melt like dumb caramel and he says, *how would I like to go out later, he knows a really nice place to eat?*

So I end up saying yes.

There is no escape. I am already in the forest of thorns.

The Hungary I loved so much has turned its face and the mystery and beauty becomes colder and harder like a lover revealing the other side of themselves. The language gets more and more complex the deeper I get into it. I am lonely.

István is honest about what he is doing and where he is going and this is when I know he isn't lying. He is working or at conferences. He is telling the truth about his life at least, but this doesn't console me. I start to wish I had never ever met him but it is too late. I don't know at this stage that it is fated for both of us, that we are addicted to each other and no amount of de-toxing will ever fix this. I have no idea that this is something I won't be able to run from, that I will keep getting thrown back into the storm however far I travel.

I'd stopped all my medication for three whole months over the summer but now I can't sleep due to obsessing over István. The last batch of pills was making my hair fall out. There's no way I am taking that anti-depressant again. I find a doctor who is happy to write me scripts for a good combination of benzos, mood stabilisers and anti-depressants. It knocks me out; literally. When I take them, an hour later I will fall off my chair unless I am in bed. I am content that the Hungarian doctors I see are happy to hand out pills like candy, no question.

There is always a problem with the prescriptions. For some reason everything is difficult in Hungary. My doctor's scripts are usually rejected by five or six pharmacies until I can find one that accepts them. And it is never the same one. If it's a Tuesday, one pharmacy says they can't take cards before midday, another says they can't give me two boxes of 100 mg tablets as I have prescription for 200mg, or the brand name is different despite the active ingredient being the same. The pharmacists all cluster round their computer and say "Nem" when I am trying to explain this. But what am I supposed to do? By the time I get to the last pharmacy I really need an anti-depressant due to all the stress.

It is December when I announce I am away to Tenerife and I am not coming back. For once I see a flicker of pain in István's beautiful eyes. "But why?" he wants to know. "I thought you were happy here." *With me,* he might as well have added as he is taking it personally.

In truth I have realised he is addicted and now and then tries to break his addiction to me by not seeing me, swearing off my body and the evil drug it has become, relishing the detox as though he is in complete control.

Which he is not; Fate is in complete control. It has mapped out our destiny for us. We can do nothing. I also think I am in control by leaving him to go to work in other countries now and then. I don't realise that Fate will drag me back to Hungary every single time I leave.

Love is blindness.

It's still not enough for him to remember our last date in the restaurant I am waiting in. I am fucking furious. His phone is switched off. I go to his apartment and the lights are all out. No one is home.

Fuck him. I can't sleep as I am so hurt and angry.

Next morning I stride into the dental surgery with his favourite chocolates. A chocoholic dentist seems a contradiction. Pity they are not hard centres as I hurl them at him one by one, livening up a boring meeting all the staff are in. They are coffee creams and they splatter him and the walls. One of the dental assistants is looking at the floor and trying not to laugh at his humiliation. This should make him mad, but no, he is afraid, running after me like a lost puppy.

He follows me to the door for once not angry, more scared I am walking away for good.

"I am so fucking angry," I tell him.

"I'm sorry," he says. "I was stupid, I was treating a patient in the hospital, she had attempted suicide under a car and her face needed so much work and I forgot the time and I was so tired......."

"Oh you weren't just stupid," I say. "You were fucking stupid. If only you had called, told me you were working late I would have understood. You hurt me so much when I was sitting in the restaurant looking like an idiot, thinking you just didn't care and then I have to take pills to sleep thinking you hate me. I am so mad. You are so selfish."

I can't help thinking the suicide girl under the wheels of a car could so easily have been me, could so easily only yesterday, only tomorrow. Only a fragile skin separates the will to live and the will to die, quivering and unstable. The fragile skin is almost translucent right now.

He raises his eyes and looks like I stabbed him through the heart. "I'm so sorry, my lady," he says.

I storm out.

"I'll call you as soon as this meeting finishes," he says.

"Don't ever call me again!" I yell. "I hate you, István! I really hate you!"

He stands with such pain in his eyes and I am glad after all the sleepless nights he caused me, that he is hurting. If only for a minute he is stabbed through the heart.

I am shaking with rage and hurt and lack of sleep that even three valium couldn't sort out last night.

I am so sick and tired of his 'forgive me I was so tired'.

I am tired, we are all tired and I am just plain tired of his excuses. So he was tired; he could have asked me over to his apartment and we could both be tired together, but no he doesn't think.

Of course when he's outside my apartment begging forgiveness an hour later I am unable to send him away. I can't as he won't leave; he keeps pleading and knocking the door until I finally give in to my stupid heart.

"My darling lady, I'm so sorry." He kisses my hands and my face. "Please forgive me, please. I am not leaving this door until you forgive me."

I shouldn't but I do. I should shower him in olives from the balcony like I will do later with an István lookalike I meet in Spain.

I feel bad treating him like this when he was fixing a suicidal girl's smashed up face for hours in the operating theatre. I tell him I am sorry, he was kind to help this girl. But István still doesn't take me to his bed and it has been six months since I met him I think so I assume he was never really interested. Maybe I was just a bit of light entertainment, maybe he is inadequate, whatever the reason I am hurt. I want to ask him but I decide not to, in case he says he is not attracted to me. I can't deal with this rejection. Not now when I am in so deep.

I am walking away and then I turn around in the cold December air and half-drunk I think, *Oh what the Hell* and I run back to him. "Take me home with you, please. Take me with you."

He smiles a beautiful smile. "Come on then, my darling lady."

I regret it almost as soon as we are in his bedroom

as he is so shy and doesn't want to get undressed despite his perfect body and I wonder if he is just inadequate. He slides into bed and turns out the light leaving the candles flickering as he looks at me and tells me I am beautiful. He ghosts a hand along the skin on my arm, then all at once he is passion personified and he pins me to the bed. He is certainly not inadequate. I let myself drown. He keeps going on about being King István again and I am his Queen. I am dying in a state of ecstasy and this is just too good. His flesh, my flesh and the world could just end right now, just don't stop, never let me go. *He is the best lover I have ever had and his creamy skin flawless and as I bury my hands in the soft black curls that hang over his face and inhale his skin, I could just die right now but I am starting to worry about these fantasies as that night he is shouting it all out in his sleep in Hungarian.*

"Father, I have finally found her, I can't let her go! She is here!" and then the rest all slurred so I am not sure what he is saying. It is a little bit freaky and I have to turn on the bedside light and hold him to stop him shouting and twisting around the sheets. His face is damp with sweat and nightmares and he calms down and holds me.

I should have left, I shouldn't be here, it is too good, too intense and also too fucking strange with this King fantasy. It will hurt both of us when I have to leave. My flight is on Monday afternoon. I stay in his bed from Saturday night until Monday morning apart from getting up to eat the takeaways he orders but he can't be away from the bedroom for long. He wants me back there with him and he wants to drink my flesh, he says. It is just too intense, too good. It feels like time stopped or stretched out into infinity like my rubbery

Salvador Dali clock.

He is shouting so much on Sunday in his sleep he actually leaps out of bed and goes over to the window and opens it and holds his arms up in the moonlight.

I laugh as I think he is playing around. He is going on about King István again and I still think it is a joke. It is only when I go over to him and he is standing with the freezing winter air whistling through the window and he is in a trance with his eyes open and they are so black as though his body is stripped of his soul. He is not there.

I am afraid. I have never seen anyone sleepwalking like this and he is oblivious to me, to the cold and the icy December wind which rushes through the bedroom, as he stands there only in boxer shorts rambling about the King. I close the window, take his arm and gently turn him round and take him back to the bed. He follows me with glassy eyes, he is a man possessed. I put on the night light and he climbs into bed and I wrap him in the duvet. The light calms him. He closes his eyes and moves close. He is back in his body.

"It's okay, honey," I say. "I am here, your Queen is here."

He murmurs and wraps himself around me and twists his hands in my hair, nestling into my chest like a child. He quietens down. I can't sleep at all after this, I feel I have to take care of him and stroke his hair, watch over his bad dreams. I kiss his delicate hands, caress his face. He is so beautiful. I only hope I can hang on to him for longer than five minutes.

My poor darling. This has been going on for a long time, I know.

I am really disturbed by this and wonder if this is why he couldn't let me into his life any sooner.

I don't mention it the next day, as he doesn't seem affected and I don't want to embarrass him. He gives me a leaving present of a beautiful sapphire necklace that Monday morning and says he will be waiting for me to come back. He holds back the long waves of my hair and drapes it around my neck as we stand before the mirror and I look into my dark brown eyes which hold so many secrets and so much pain and I feel a strange sense of infinity ghosting across our reflections. I put it down to the intensity of the weekend as I think, *what a shame. We look so beautiful together.*

He smiles at us in the mirror. He will light a candle every day I am away and he will be waiting.

He thinks he is going to see me again. He doesn't act like this is the end. I believe it is the end.

I will not come back. This is what I think. I don't tell him this but in my heart I am so sad. Part of this is because I am too afraid to tell him what I really want, and I am too afraid he will leave me first so again, as I always do I have to do the leaving. I think of the image of us together and it as though my beauty is not enough alone. Together we are beautiful. We look so good in the mirror and alone, I never feel beautiful. Maybe his presence makes me glow because of the happiness I feel to be next to him but I know I am not complete without him.

Physically he is so perfect even down to his delicate hands which are designed for painting the most accurate of masterpieces or performing neurosurgery. He is messed up but who am I to judge, maybe he should have been a writer or artist and his dreams are just a way of his creativity manifesting itself. He is working in science so maybe he needs this expression in his subconscious world.

Do I really care if he is bipolar or even schizophrenic? At this stage I have to say I am in so deep that I would love him if he were a serial killer. I am hopelessly and totally in love with him I don't know what to do with everything I am feeling.

Maybe he is just having very creative dreams like I do where I dream in full Futurist swirling colours and wild movement and they are brilliantly intense, coloured by the palette of a dazzling artist.

I hope.

VODKA

**Crystalline fire
Glacier pure
Burns a path
Seeking pain to obliterate
Oblivion
My water of Life
And Death
Murder me now**

I am fucked up beyond belief. I cry all the way to Tenerife, half-wishing I hadn't got on the plane, but I was too proud to talk to István and tell him what I was really feeling and tell him that I wanted to stay with him, through the dark winter and never leave. I go manic in the heat and more than a few times I am in some bar with a load of travellers drinking beer after wine, washing down my meds with more wine. I get demon migraines and pop more codeine pills to sort those out. I even cut some of my valium into lines and snort it like cocaine to get more of a hit to numb the pain of everything. Fuck it all. Is this what my life has become? 4000 kilometres away from the love of my life. What the Hell am I doing? Why didn't I just tell him what I wanted? It was so sweet and intense, it isn't as if we didn't end our weekend on the best possible note. But I know from experience that I cannot trust my damaged heart and I cannot trust men. *How many wonderful loving weekends turn to nothing in the end once we part? All, in my experience. Why would this be different.*

I take a Binter Canarias flight to Fuerteventura trying to escape myself and rent a cheap holiday apartment. I am not escaping anything, if at all I am running further into the fire. The flames are stronger here on this barren island. I drink champagne vodka cocktails I mix in the apartment as the bar is so dire and stuffed with bulging Brits drinking all day and night. They will not leave me alone. I am wearing a diamond and a wedding ring on my right hand as they do in Eastern Europe and I tell the losers who hit on me every time I want a bit of relaxation by the pool or early evening in the bar that I am married to a Hungarian mafia man. This would command respect in the East where even the drunkest Russian or Hungarian has stepped back and apologised.

The Western response is "Well, why isn't he here?"

Maybe he doesn't like the sun, maybe he is busy working to give me a nice life, maybe he doesn't get seasonal affective disorder like I do but whatever the reason or the lie is it is none of their fucking business.

And it doesn't mean I am available.

One night a Geordie man is hammering at my door as I hide in the bathtub. The doors are so weak they could break off their hinges. Even I could kick that door in.

What is wrong with these people??Does the word mafia mean nothing or are they just dumb?

I hate the West even more after this and I know my world now lies in Eastern Europe.

But my love hasn't called me. It obviously was nothing to him. How do men do that? Make you feel wonderful and then forget you immediately. But I touch the sapphires round my neck and they speak a different story; one of beauty and eternity not rejection and jealousy. The cold jewels are a reminder that maybe I should just trust this man, if only halfway.

I watch Italian gameshows, trash Spanish TV and spend evenings snorting lines of valium or klonopin, drinking all the time. I tie a ligature around my neck and pull it until I see stars. This is it, this is the end. I am half conscious and life has become way too much. Each time I tighten the knot and nearly black out and then loosen it again, my body is getting weaker. I can hardly untie the knot the last time, I could easily just sleep now and I will not wake up. Guaranteed. I picture everyone I know around me not urging me to stop but urging me to do it. This is how messed up my head is. I really believe they are in the room telling me to kill myself.

I can't control the depression, the mania, the mood swings. Twenty years of it, and I should be a veteran bipolar by now but no, I have tried everything; drinking, not drinking, coffee, no coffee, sleep, no sleep, eating, not eating and pills or no pills, working hard, not working hard but whatever I do I am fighting a demon that is just way too much for me. And István hasn't called. I think that maybe I was just a brief wonder. But why buy me this sapphire necklace. I can't die and not know the answers. I think of him and again, I touch the stones around my neck and I know I can't die and not know the answer to him and his heart.

What stops me ending it all that night, as I am losing consciousness and blacking out?

Once I touch the necklace as I lie halfway between life and death, I have to get up. I decide I can't die without cleaning my teeth and once in the bathroom I realise I am so tired, due to all the alcohol, pills and lack of oxygen and all I can do is climb into bed. I look in the mirror and touch the cold jewels and the pale tiny scar by my right ear, where he opened me up to find my flesh and bone and heal it with his love. Then I feel bad. To die after all he has done is ungrateful. I have to get out of this island. It's nothing but a desert with more goats than people.

And I'm tired of being hauled out of the tropical plants by the security guard every evening when I have fallen over outside my apartment drunk and am unable to get up. That night I pick up the phone and dial his number. It is midnight but he answers gently, without frustration.

"I need you," I say. "I'm sorry but I need you." I am crying.

"Hey, baby," he says gently. "It is okay to need somebody. When are you coming home? Maybe I need you too."

The connection is clear across the 4,000 kilometres.

"Just come back, come back soon," he tells me. "Sweet dreams."

And then he is gone. Disappearing into his nightmares and his other world.

What happened to me? I had such high hopes. I remember when I was four years old I dressed up as Wonder Woman for the school fancy dress competition. My mother spent so long sewing stars and stripes and setting my hair that when we arrived, the Incredible Hulk had won and was bouncing on a trampoline with his trophy. I felt that first feeling of being cheated out of what I deserved, forever to be too late, second best, shit out of luck when it came to job interviews, love, you name it, I am the unluckiest person I know. Which makes me run from all the pain across Europe and into what I hope is a better life, only it is not turning out that way the past few years. The same bad luck, the nearly, the maybes and the *could have beens* and not through lack of trying.

I need someone to take care of me. No one ever took care of me and I was always so independent, but I know despite my independent spirit and my confident air, I need a man like István to take care of me. No, not like him; exactly him.

I need him. And I am too afraid to admit it even to myself. Which is why I am drinking and pill-popping for my sanity or insanity. His face drifts in front of me when I am sober or wrecked and I know there is no escape. I have to go back, I have to find out the answer to my István, even if it means risking heartbreak. I am always running away from someone or something and he is the most beautiful man I have ever met and I would regret this for the rest of my life if we had a chance of happiness together and I never took it through fear and mistrust.

I have told him I need him and he is not afraid. I have to take the step into the forest of thorns but for now I only see the roses, beautiful and delicate. So I put my fear aside and I drift in.

Kiára Árgenta

SZERET

Powder
Candy
Crack cocaine
I inhale your skin
Sweet peppermint gasoline
It burns

My heart will explode

You have climbed in there
And reshaped everything
Melted the metal, the steel furnace of emotion
Into something more malleable
And manageable

I can do nothing
But admire your beauty
Drink you in; your hair, your eyes, your flesh,
With spun sugar
My absinthe
As though it's my last night on earth

I whisper your name
Mystic music
And the sound stretches through infinity

Of course I am back in Hungary on 17th January.
István suggests I help him with some marketing in
the surgery, since I speak Italian and French we could
do with some rich Swiss patients. He said he needs a
good multilingual speaker since he spends half his
week at the hospital. He hands me a uniform, he

wants me to represent his business. This does not make me popular amongst the other girls as I am still no way up to standard with my Hungarian and they are resentful. They know about us, it is all too obvious and they don't like it. They don't want him as a man; I sense it is not jealousy in this way. If anything, they would never want him. I pick this up from the way they look at him and the conversations I overhear while pretending not to understand. I hear the practice manager telling one of the dental assistants she wouldn't want to go out with him in a million years. This is not what I expect as he is rich, devastatingly handsome and charming but yet there is a warning sign he wears like a dark cold aura and these Hungarian girls recognise it and I do not, being an alien in this country.

István also doesn't want me running off again, is keen to anchor me somehow. I am straight into his apartment again the first day I am back and he starts to suck my blood from bites he makes in my shoulders. I am a little messed up by this, as he was so gentle the first time I stayed with him that weekend before Christmas. Tonight is just a precursor of what is to come. He is sorry he says the next morning. He missed me and my beautiful flesh. It is so lovely, he can't help himself and he kisses the bite marks and keeps saying sorry. He says he is sorry he didn't call me much over the holiday time as he was so scared I might never come back and his heart would explode with grief.

That is intense after such a short time; I like it. No, I love it.

As I trace the outlines of his perfect face, those beautiful black eyelashes close in happiness and I realise I have let myself fall way further than I ever did before. I love him so totally I can do nothing.

I wonder if he was with someone else, but try as hard as I can I can find no evidence in his apartment and I am an expert in cheating. I know men are careless and there is nothing to suggest he has done anything other than work and sleep. He is honest and I trust my instincts.

Working with him drives us both over the edge in a bittersweet way. I am happy to see more of him and he likes me around but his raging jealousy and controlling nature clashes with my volcanic temperament. He calls me "Fucking volcano girl," making reference to my split nationality with the Sicilian and Icelandic rocky lands of fire and ice.

He has no idea I tried to kill myself in Spain only a couple of weeks' ago. I would never want him to know this. It is only much later when I am sure he will not leave me, or judge me that I admit to it and he can hold me and let me tell him what demons I have fought with for 20 years and have to fight every waking moment and day. He doesn't know I am bipolar. I want to tell him but I am afraid he will leave me. I hide my pills but I can't hide my mood swings.

But for now, he just thinks I am moody and difficult and we scream in the dental surgery in front of the other staff, we scream at each other in restaurants, we shout on phones, in cars. We have a food fight in one restaurant when we are in Budapest one weekend. It's an expensive Italian place and the staff don't throw us out, maybe because they know István has plenty of money to burn, maybe because it gives the staff a bit of light relief on a Saturday night. The other diners are also listening as we argue half in English, half in Hungarian and maybe it livens up their evenings. I am too mad to be embarrassed. He races us back to Pécs at 200 kmph that night. We are both burning with anger, the limoncello has given him indigestion and I have tiramisu in my hair and neither of us is wearing a seatbelt. It's zero drink driving in Hungary and yet here he is drink driving shooting through the centre of the road with a crazy look in his eyes. If we hit anyone he will go to prison unless he bribes the police with a load of cash. Here love and hate are hopelessly fused.

"Are you scared, baby?" he glances at me with a sarcastic look. The cobra has moved in and it flickers through his dark expression.

I guess many women would be screaming by now. I do not care.

"No, I am not afraid of death," I say looking at him.

He looks at me again, his eyes darken and he accelerates harder into the darkness.

I pull his curls and stick my nails in the back of his neck when he complains of a headache. I am angry too. Getting nice seems to get me nowhere. He tells me I am strange, really fucking strange. I tell him to take a good look at himself and stop hiding behind everything. I never mention his King of Hungary, that constant refrain and nightmare when he is asleep. I am scared he will lock me out of his life forever for seeing too much.

"I'm just different," he says arrogantly.

"No, mister," I tell him. "You are as strange as me." I am thinking of last night when he was calling his army to battle and asking was his horse ready in that dream. It could be funny, except it isn't. I have read up about this historic István, the first king of Hungary and I don't know why my man is having these dreams, whether he is schizophrenic or bipolar one and really believes he is the King or whether he has just had a childhood fantasy which no one ever stopped him having. He won't answer when I ask about his parents. I am not asking to meet them, I am just curious as to what they do and why he chose a medical career. But he will not answer. I don't push it. I wonder if he argued with them and then never spoke again. I don't know.

"You're not normal," he continues. "And stop pulling my fucking hair." He swerves on the road.

"You want normal?" I shout. "You told me you liked me because I was different, you said you never met anyone like me in your life."

He doesn't answer. And he never says anything nice anymore such as 'You look pretty today/tonight'.

I tell him he looks very nice, handsome and he just says 'Thank you'.

I start to doubt if I look nice at all and eat less and less as I am stressed.

My bones are sticking through my back, my collarbones are like coat hangers and I know I must be too thin as people are always telling me "Please, eat something. Anything."

One friend shoves me in a chair and pushes chocolate in my mouth as if I am a famine victim. This must be bad. However, I can't see it. I feel on the chunky side of normal and protruding bones must mean I am big boned. My mother has offered to pay for the Priory. This must be really bad. But I still cannot see it.

Despite our fine cuisine and expensive restaurants, I am not eating a fraction of it. István happily eats three courses while I toy with one starter and plenty of wine. He doesn't comment too much but he does say "Baby, you are too thin". He doesn't push it though. I just take it as a compliment, being too thin. It is like someone telling me I am beautiful. Which he never does any more. In fact I only recall him saying it once. But he tells me I have this amazing energy about me which lifts my beauty to the highest level. "It's a *want to fuck* energy," he tries to explain. "Like your body is constantly smouldering like a volcano." It sounds kind of crude as he puts it that way. But as he looks at me with his lovely dark eyes, I know he doesn't mean it to be crude. It's when he speaks English, he overuses the word 'fuck'. Maybe we should just speak in Hungarian.

I realise when I mention some nights later in a restaurant that I have sampled the tastes of every European nation and a few transatlantic and southern hemispheres too and I don't mean food, that I have said too much. István looks at me like I am a whore. He has not had the range of experience I have had, despite having ten years on me but the idea of casual sex seems to fill him with disgust.

He is angry and I have to say something to mitigate what I have just said.

"But that was a long time ago, I don't think like that any longer and I look at you and I see infinity. I don't want another man as long as I live, only you. All the others, they were nothing compared to you. You could line up all the Hollywood stars and I would walk past them and straight to you."

His mouth splits into a smile. He likes that.

"You are the most beautiful man on earth," I continue, as I am drunk. But what I say when I am drunk is always true. I mean it. I don't want the richest, the most glittering stars the world could offer me. I want this Hungarian dentist with his beauty and his strange way of thinking and him and only him. I want the pain and the ecstasy. I want it all, all the time.

"No, sure I'm not," he says but he is happy.

"Yes," I insist. "The most beautiful man I could ever find even if I searched every corner of the globe. I could look at you all night"

I am intensely honest when I have a drink. Most people find it too much when I am sober.

My food is hardly touched on my plate. I am a terrible eater; I push it around and talk and drink wine and then realise I am not hungry anyway. I am a very cheap date in this way.

I ask him what is his blood group and before he tells me, I already know the answer; O negative.

Same as me.

He is the first person not to ask *Why the Hell are you asking me that? Nutcase.*

He just answers matter of fact. But he is Hungarian, he is also strange and he doesn't see it as a strange question.

"You're in my blood, baby," he smiles.

I feel I have found my other self.

But he still says *that I am strange, really strange and that he has never met anyone like me.*

I tell him I have found my other self. This lights up his eyes like a thousand years of waiting and he says *he knows it; he will never let me go.*

"I will never let you go, Kiára. Not as long as I live and breathe."

I am dizzy with the intensity of it all.

That night, the 21st January is supposed to be one of the most depressing days of the year when everyone feels miserable, but not for me this time. He carries me into his bedroom and says *he is drinking in my flesh like the finest champagne, he says he wants to devour me and my body and drink the sweet blood that flows through my veins. He has been waiting for this moment a long, long time. He wanted me to know that, he wanted it to be special. He wanted me to know he was serious about me. He doesn't want anyone else, he says. There is no one else. He was waiting 6 months for me to go to his bedroom. He wanted to do this the day he met me but that isn't how he treats a lady and when I was with him in his bed before Christmas he felt he couldn't let himself go as he was scared I wouldn't come back to Hungary and he would end up with a knife in his heart. He would have lost his Queen.*

So he is vulnerable, I think. All the same, I am puzzled by the not letting himself go comment. He seemed to let himself go that weekend in December. Yes, I had to ask him to take me to his bedroom but he seemed to lose his inhibitions after that and was passionate and loving. He was also happy when I got back from the Canary Islands and seemed passionate that night.

So what exactly does he mean if that isn't letting go?

I realise after the other night and those preliminary bites what he means. He has some strange behaviour in bed, the nightmares aside. If I wasn't drunk, I would think he was a vampire. He covers my back in bites and at one point his sharp teeth do puncture my shoulder, deeper than before and he sucks hard on the wound. I like the pain and I like the hurt. He is drinking my blood.

I wonder if I have died at some point this night or if I have inadvertently taken crack, or smack or some drug which is making me feel in such a state of unearthly ecstasy. The pain of the bite gives way to the best orgasm of my life and I start to wonder if he spiked my drink or food in the restaurant but then he wouldn't. Why wait 6 months to take someone home in the first place and then spike their drink the third time you are with them?

God, I am dying with happiness. If I die tonight I would die happy.

When I get up to go to the bathroom later I am shocked to see my back is covered in violet bruises and teeth marks.

A Hungarian vampire dentist. Maybe he really is a vampire. My shoulder has a puncture wound like a snake bite and it is looking so bad and I worry my bites will get infected. But it feels so good to hurt without self-harming. I have finally found my solution after 20 years of cutting and burning.

That is not socially acceptable but this is. He also has never judged me like everyone else for my self-harm. He doesn't like it, but it has never put him off me. He is the one man who stands up against all the others who run away or threaten 'If you do that again, I am leaving you.'

Look what you've done, I say to him snapping on the bedside lamp.

He is half asleep and scratchy about being woken up.

"What?" he snarls. "What is so important it can't wait until tomorrow, I've got a busy day in surgery and I need my sleep."

There is blood on his lips as he is sitting up in the bed. There is a drop of blood on his chin; my blood. He is a fucking vampire, a devastatingly handsome vampire. A springy black curl hangs down his forehead and his eyes are so black I can't see the pupils. I don't care if he devours me right now and I join the undead. In fact, I hope he will. I never want to get out of this bed.

I show him my back and he gasps.

"I didn't do that," he says shocked.

"Well I can't reach my back with my own teeth," I say. Sure, I am bendy as a former gymnast but I still can't do this circus trick.

He touches it with his soft hands.

"Oh, darling, my darling lady, I am so sorry. Your flesh is just so beautiful, I couldn't help myself; the smell and taste of your skin so sweet."

"Vampire dentist," I say out loud.

He kisses the bites so gently and lays me down on my side and then goes and gets some antiseptic wipes from his bathroom cabinet.

Bipolar too, I think. His moods are so volatile and he is hiding them from me less and less. I wonder if his bipolar condition is leading to the King of Hungary fantasies. I have realised he is not schizophrenic but I know for sure he is bipolar.

I have to hide my illness from him, hide my pills as I am scared he will run away if he knows about me. When he first met me I had to show him some antidepressants I was taking as they could have a reaction with the local anaesthetic injections. He was shocked and told me I shouldn't take this poison and I promised I didn't really need it and was coming off them. If only he knew the truth.

He thinks I am pill-free now. I hide my stash so well.

I should get out now but I can't. I am a junkie. I feel like he has shot me up with heroin. I turn around and kiss him and I am addicted. He is now in my blood, I bite his lips and taste his blood and this is us, entwined for good. We have little sleep that night. We have no control. It isn't the same as the holding back in December, there is no control, there is no holding back for either of us. I scratch my claws into his back so hard his flesh is under my fingernails. He is ecstatic with exquisite pain and pleasure both and his eyes, his endless dark eyes look at me until he holds me down and bites me again, this time over my heart.

I love it. I am in love with him. I am dying in ecstasy. If this is Heaven, I am happy I found it.

He is unresponsive and moody over breakfast and I wonder if it is the same István; this will be the pattern for a long time. He makes me my coffee and freshly-squeezed juice without a word and slaps down a croissant on the breakfast table. He doesn't like my sweet breakfasts and makes himself something savoury with vegetable juices to go with it. I am touched he has all the food I like in the morning ready for me and I try to give him a hug but he pushes me away, without a word and without looking at me. I say nothing. I don't want to start an argument now. I sit down and eat my breakfast while he angrily washes up, smacking the plates around so hard some break in the bowl and he curses "Baszd meg".

Then to show he is in control, he decides to swear off the drug that is me for a few days or even a week and it drives us both crazy, especially since I am working in his surgery and every tiny brush of his skin against mine leaves us both in ecstasy and trapped desire. He looks like a drowning man when he has told me he is busy for the weekend with conferences then his skin brushes mine as I reach for the coffee or something and his eyes grow large and he holds his chest as though his heart is hurting him and hurries away into a treatment room. It is easier when he is in the hospital I can concentrate better without him, as he does without me. Together we are hopeless junkies needing our next fix and the next into eternity, forever chasing that elusive rainbow.

Why do I attract strange types? *Why can't he just be normal?*

"You are a bit strange yourself, Kiára," my friend Katalin says. "Are you sure Ernő Rubik isn't your dad?"

"It's this difficult language," I say. "It is fucking with my head like a Rubik cube. Plus these middle-aged Hungarian men think in a weird way."

"No, it's just the ones you attract," she says. "Find someone younger, more normal."

I remember the last time Katalin set me up with two of her male friends my age. I asked them did they live together as the three of us were sitting in a bar and they yelled "We're not fucking queer!" throwing their pálinka glasses to the floor.

One grabs a pair of scissors and cuts off a lock of my hair telling me he's a magician and will perform spells on it to make me want him. The other chases me out of the bar shouting "Give me your tongue! I want your tongue!"

As I said, Rubik cubes.

This is impossible. Normal equates boring. It wouldn't last five minutes. My shrink was trying to explain to me once that 'grey is good'. I was asking why life had to be Heaven or Hell, up or down, black or white and nothing in the middle.

"It can be. Remember, that grey is good."

I remember the shrink's words but I can't live by them. They make sense but I have already thrown the guidebook and the map away and plunged into the forest of thorns for pain and for pleasure.

Screw the shrink and his fortune cookie psychology.

I have some interviews for an advertising job in

Kiev on Skype. István has sworn off the sins of the flesh for a week and I am going nuts. This includes no visits to his apartment and not much talking. I cannot deal with this control freak business. I yell at István I am going to Ukraine, what is one cold-hearted European country compared to another. This threat hangs over him as I nearly get the job. For once he is chewed up, asking me every day have I heard anything from Kiev. I don't get the job and he is so relieved. I would have gone if I got it and in a way I am relieved when I hear his sigh of relief. "Good," he says. "Good". He is so relieved he closes his eyes as if to thank someone or some entity.

But he forgets my fucking birthday all the same. It's on April the first. I am the April fool. I even make a point of telling him the week before and he says Happy Birthday for next week. I ask him to take me out. He says he will try.

No apology. I hate him. I don't even mention it. *What's the matter?* he wants to know when I don't look at him the next day.

"Nothing," I say. "Nothing at all."

"Oh," he says and carries on getting changed in the staffroom. I look at his lovely torso which is fleshy but toned as he is looking down and I think, *Bastard, why are you so fucking good-looking.*

There isn't a part of him physically I would want to change.

I want to run at him and bite that chest and slap him and then embrace him all at once. He is messing with my head.

May starts out as a balanced month. We are level, no shouting, no screaming. That isn't to say we are flat-lining but it's as close to stable as I or we can get. Or this is the grey that my shrink talked about. I don't feel right. I should be on my way up or way down.

On one of the rare visits back to Llangollen and Wales I tell my uncle "Sometimes I am so angry I want to take an AK-47 and blast the street away."

He laughs as we pass a bus stop lined with people as I say this.

I take some handmade Welsh chocolates back for István. He loves to receive gifts. He always tears open the wrapper so fast like a kid at Christmas and I love to see the delight in his face. However mad I am at him, however hopeless he has been about calling me, however moody he has been, the childish happiness is priceless. I love to see him smile; a thousand years of rainbows in that face when he likes my gifts. He takes me back to his apartment more and more but he behaves like a man possessed. *I am a drug* he tells me in bed *and he can't stop. I am in his blood. It is too late for us now.* This last remark sounds really weird.

Too late for what? For once I am not enjoying the night. I have a headache. I tell him this contraceptive pill is giving me constant headaches, sometimes the migraines are so bad I feel as though my skull will split but I never say "Not tonight, István, I have a headache." I still want him to fuck me. Even if my head explodes.

"Stop taking it then," he tells me.

"What do I use instead? I don't like condoms," I say. "And the IUD gives me awful pain."

"I don't like condoms either. So the answer is nothing, we use nothing." He is matter of fact.

"That is not a good plan," I tell him to his back.

"It's fine with me if you stop your pill," he says into the darkness.

I trace a finger down his perfect spine which makes

him shiver.

Neither of us has said we love each other yet. I wonder if he can love. I wonder if he is too damaged to love. Either way, I can't say it first and neither can he.

That is not a good plan. I will just have to have headaches. I can't believe the fact that no contraception doesn't worry him in the slightest given his controlling nature. I thought he would hate the idea of kids. It is not something we ever discussed but given he never married and never had any of his own, I thought he hated them.

After another bad headache he tells me to stop taking the pill. I am lying in bed with a bag of milk over my head to stop the migraine. I always found this a novelty when I first saw them in Hungary, these bagged litres of milk. He takes the bag of milk off my head and says, this is it, that contraceptive pill stops today. If I have a baby that is fine but he is not going to watch me suffer like this and these headaches could end up in a stroke or heart attack.

"Besides," he says. "A baby would be good for you. You need to have a child to look after. It is what you need in your life. Stop you worrying about yourself and getting depressed."

I can't argue, my head hurts too much.

He is a doctor, he says and I need to stop, it is poison. And it is time I had a baby. I need to think about the future. I need a focus. He scoops up my stash of the pill and throws them in the trash.

So I do stop the pill. I only hope he knows what he is doing. He tells me he knows what he is doing and this is the time for both of us. He strokes my headache away with his cool fingers like a magician and I will do anything he says.

I never have any sense. And there is no love

between us that is spoken of, only the searing passion once the lights are out. I am afraid for the future and maybe I am stupid for listening to him.

The balanced month doesn't last. After a night of tenderness, he is soft and kind over breakfast and he serves me my favourite pastries and I think maybe we are on to a good thing here. In work later, a switch snaps out the man from only an hour ago into abrupt and cold and just plain nasty and I snarl at him, "what is wrong with you today?" and slam the office door. This should be the end of the conversation.

He explodes. So much for me being the volcano.

He yells the immortal line "You like what we do here, good! You don't like it, also *good!*" His dark eyes are jet black. He is changing for a conference and he opens the office door dressed only in his underwear. It could be funny except it isn't.

I try to take his arm and tell him I'm sorry but he shakes me off and shoves me hard. "Leave me alone! I've had it with you and your behaviour."

The next week is Hell. I have said how sorry I am and apologised no end of times but he is vicious and cruel. I tell him after a week of bullying and nastiness in early June, I am away to Madrid for 5 days as I pre-booked it. He has been horrible all week apart from when I take in a Swiss couple as my dental patients and then he is nice to me so I think everything is forgotten.

As soon as they are gone he is making comments in Hungarian to the other staff about me and laughing. I say "Értem téged." *I understand you.* I walk out of the door.

The bastard, I think. *The heartless bastard. And I stopped taking my goddamn contraceptive.*

He is so dominant the staff are having to pretend to laugh and agree with what he says about 'az Angol lány'.

I know they are just afraid of arguing with him and his bullying. I shout as I leave in Hungarian that "I am not the English girl. I have no drop of English blood in me. I am Welsh, Icelandic and Sicilian and fuck you, István for not knowing the difference. Do you think that Hungarians are Austrians?"

Is Hungarian anything like German, you idiot?

I have already run back to his apartment and I am packing up my stuff to leave when he arrives and yells at me for showing him up in front of his staff and I tell him he did that himself.

He tries to take my passport and tells me I can't leave the country. I ask him why does he want me around since he is so nasty to me? He smiles and says he wants me around, I can't leave him.

But he is extremely angry with me for shouting at him in the surgery, no one has talked to him this way, not even his own mother. He is not sure if he can forgive me.

I want to say that I could have said things a thousand times worse, he hasn't seen anything of the volcano yet and maybe his mother should have spoken to him like that and not treated him like the God he thinks he has become. He is a spoilt only child and it shows.

He says *he will drive me back to my apartment.*

As I get out of his car, he grabs my arm and orders me to smile for him. His eyes are full of danger and sarcasm and his grip is hurting. I smile.

"No, darling," he says. "A real smile and then you can get out." He won't let go and his nails dig into my skin.

"Smile for me like a good girl." He twists my arm and smiles at me with eyes full of hate and violent jealousy.

I do as I am told so I can get out of this fucking car.

"And the rest," he orders laughing at me. I am pulling up my dress hating and loving him at the same time while he sits there looking at me with glazed eyes and he says, *that I am just made for sex. I am a good girl. I do what he says.*

He then gently strokes the scar on my jawbone and says, "You will always come back to me, Kiára, I know it."

Afterwards he watches me go into my apartment. I look out of the living room window and his car is still there. He is staring up into the blackness where I am. He is so strange. He sits there for about half an hour not moving. Does he want me to go down to him as he knows I can see him? Then he just drives away in his black car, tyres screeching.

Once I am in Madrid, I can't go back to Hungary. I am staying in the centre but as every tree lined fountain ended avenue looks the same it seems like an artificial city. Everything is expensive. A coffee in the roof terrace of an art gallery is five euros. The churros the hostel serves up for breakfast every morning are cold and sullen. My goddamn period is ten days late and I am afraid as I sense he is virile and healthy and now we are not speaking to each other. I feel sick in the morning but it is probably the fatty churros.

To crown the horror of the past two weeks I am having a drink in a bar with two girls from the hostel I am staying somewhere in central Madrid. My violent ex-boyfriend from Valencia walks in with a crowd of buddies. He is staring at me and laughing and all his buddies are looking over. I whisper to one of the girls, an Aussie, as I have already told her the story and she says "Don't worry, we will make sure we get home or we will call the cops."

We carry on drinking and my ex walks around no less than 20 times, this bar being in a circle and he says loudly so I can hear to one of his friends "Yes, I know that lady."

I am so shaken. Lucky he pays his tab and exits but when the three of us are leaving he obviously has watched us go back into the hostel nearby as next morning when I walk out he runs across the street towards me. I dive into a café and order breakfast and he goes past leering into the window about 10 times. I don't look up but I can see the blue of his shirt out of the corner of my eye. I want to ask the owner to call the Guardia but I am too afraid to move. I end up talking to the owner past lunchtime and well into siesta where he locks the door and we chatter about Mexico, where he is from and he gives me free Margaritas. I am so grateful but it shows that mainland Spain is not safe. I book a flight out for the next day.

What messes me up is the fact he is laughing at me. I type out a fake law bill in Russian and mail it to the last address I had for him in Valencia via a friend in Moscow and hope the strange language demanding the equivalent of 3,000 euros will stop him making contact with me. I can't use Hungarian, he can't know where I am.

My mother never understands this, she always says "Why not make him feel bad and you can live where you want." This makes me mad. She isn't the one who can never eat another apple as long as she lives and has to have constant dental work to fix the jaw or more maintain it as it can't really be fixed. Who the hell wants to see their violent ex laughing at them every time they leave the house. Especially when he has told all his friends or our friends more like, his version of events and it will not include the death threats and the smashed jaw. I know if I lived in Madrid, he would hunt me down. He has no idea I am in Eastern Europe and wouldn't know where to start looking.

Kiára Árgenta

TŰZ ÉS JÉG

I go back to my other spiritual home in the Canary Islands. I call into work and say I am sick I need to have treatment in Spain, the hospitals are very good. No one could argue with that given the state of the health service in Hungary. I tell István I am working online for now. He is probing, asking me what is wrong with me, what treatment I am having.

"Women's problems," I say. *This should shut any man up.*

But no, he keeps on. What is it? I better not be having an abortion out there. He will never forgive me.........

What do you care? I say.

I hang up.

A text arrives a minute later; **Come back. Come back to me. I miss you. I am having bad dreams and there is no one here to hold me. Kiára, come back. I forgive you everything you said to me. I am hurting if I hurt you. Just tell me you love me.**

I am drunk and it is evening and I don't know what to do with this. Of course I could say I love him but after the last two weeks he has been so horrible I don't know if he will turn as nasty as everyone else I ever trusted with my heart.

Everyone in Gran Canaria tells me not to go back to this sadist. He is treating me like dirt. How can I think of having a child with this man and being locked into him forever? But of course I find his likeness everywhere. I am not over him, never will be. He is in my blood. He was right; it is too late for us now. I am 4000 kilometres from him and I understand the true meaning of obsession which will not leave even if you travel to the end of the earth. I pick up his likeness on beaches, in bars and of course, they are not him. They have his Mediterranean looks but they are just assholes. István has his faults, at times he is a sadist but no one understands what we have together. Not even me. And I hate to think of him alone with his nightmares and night terrors. I know exactly what that is like to be afraid at night. To need someone to hold, to tell you it is okay when your night terrors are so bad you are thrown out of bed with fear and looking for demons which aren't there.

And to have the one you love more than anything to hold you and tell you it is okay is priceless.

Only no one understood me. They were not the loves of my life, just men passing through.

What are you doing down there?

I am looking under the bed for the monsters who are in my adult dreams and I am convinced something is out to get me on the top floor of an apartment block.

So I know what he is going through. And it cuts me to pieces that he is hurting alone. He is cruel, I know, but he is damaged. And he knows when he has been sadistic and he hurts inside.

Meanwhile I am writing early in the morning and drinking all night to forget. It is easy to lose yourself in paradise, or unravel. Drink and partying is cheap. It is summer all year and we are all escaping something which leads to Monday feeling like Friday or Sunday is Saturday. You don't need a reason to get wild here, you need a reason not to. This is stupid, so stupid as I am drinking to forget whereas I know he is right. I am not getting any younger. It is time I had a baby, especially with someone I love. My body is craving it but my soul is resisting it. I am still late with my time of the month and I pray it is stress. I throw up every morning, but put it down to the alcohol as there is lots of it every night. I am in denial. He is a sadist and he wouldn't care. I will end up a single mother in Spain looking after a child I couldn't get rid because of my stupid love, whilst he picks up with his new roadkill in Hungary.

I am paranoid as Hell.

István starts to leave pleading messages on my cell phone. "Where are you? Please, darling, please come to phone. Please give me a number where I can reach you. I need you. Darling I need you."

Spain is a big country and he knows I tend to disappear in its labyrinth. But he also knows I can't stay away more than so long. Especially after the burning madness where I end up blacking out under the flag of Uruguay after Mojitos and Jägerbombs and dancing on tables every night. I can't do this. One night I fall off a table drunk in my high heels and I am bleeding, there is blood on the floor and my stomach is cramping probably due to lack of food and too much alcohol. I hit my head and they call an ambulance. Everyone is completely wasted and it is something like 3 am and no one can really tell the paramedics what happened. I have had free shots of honey rum for dancing on the table and the glasses lie scattered around me, like some crazy magic circle of shot glasses and me in the middle, the sacrifice in my own altar of pain.

I have lost the ability to speak English let alone Spanish as I am out of it but once in hospital they tell me the blood is not from my head but I am having a miscarriage. I am fucked up and cry alone. The kind Spanish medics all keep coming over and asking me can they call my boyfriend. They assume he is

Spanish as I speak to them in Spanish, they are kinder as they don't see me as a drunken stupid Brit with my looks and my language. They think he will just come to the hospital. But he is 4000km away and immersed in teeth and would he care anyway now? I say he is in Hungary, it is too far and I don't know if he would care we didn't exactly part on good terms when I came to Spain. A kind nurse says she would call him for me but she speaks no English so this is no good.

When I travel back to Hungary it takes me 21 hours. I have to wait 10 hours in Bergamo and I am manic the next day when I go into work at the dental surgery in Pécs to see István and it's nearly 40c and within 2 minutes we are arguing again, this time about money. We don't know what to do with each other. "So, back in Hungary, are we," he gloats when I arrive. *I am in no mood, or more like I am manic as hell. I haven't told him about the miscarriage, he is not in a caring mood. It is only a week later and I am still fragile, I have to run to the toilets and cry. He has no idea. I hunch down into a ball on the floor and howl.*

The days are full of arguments and the hot nights are full of burning passion that knows no limits, no stopping and no safety. We hurt each other physically and emotionally. He flirts with women in front of me and I in turn flirt with younger men only he loses complete control when I do this whereas I can bottle my hurt, save it until I am alone. He goes up to whichever man I smile at and tells him in Hungarian I am his. He hates me talking to good looking patients in the surgery. I am just doing my job at times as they are my Swiss patients. Afterwards he says to me "Bet you wanted to fuck him, you were acting like a tart." Or something like this.

I tell him I have no control over whether the patients are ugly or attractive. Does he want me to screen them so only ugly men can come to his surgery?

One day soon after I get back, I cannot stop crying. I cry in work for hours, salt dripping into my keyboard and a dental assistant goes to fetch him. My hormones are all over the place.

He sits down opposite me and I look down afraid to show my weakness.

"Hey, life isn't so bad, darling, why are you crying?" He is sorry if he has said something to upset me. He reaches across the table for my hand. I tell him about the miscarriage in Spain, and I fell off the table and the medics wanted me to call him and I couldn't as I did not know if he would care given the way we argued before I left. I put my head on my computer and cry harder.

I didn't think he cared, I tell him, *I thought he hated me.*

"Baby, why didn't you tell me?" He is out of his chair and pressing my face into his dental whites where I leave spiders of mascara. "Oh, my poor little girl, you went through that all alone."

He is so hurt I didn't tell him. His eyes look like they are full of tears and he promises he will take me home early, we will talk. He chokes on his emotions and hurries out of the room. He does not want me to see he is so upset.

He forgets of course, forgets I am there, immersed as he is in his surgery and it is 9pm and I am sitting frozen to my chair when he finally comes in. I could sit here all night as I am paralysed with grief and pain that I didn't think I would feel. My body is full of hormones I don't want or understand as this has not happened to me before. He is sorry, he lost track of time and we ride home in silence. His nasty streak is latent as he carries me to his bed and wants to know how, when, what happened and why didn't I call him. I am beyond talking and he wraps me in his arms telling me he is sorry, so sorry but it can happen the first time, but no problem it shows my body is not infertile; it is a good sign for the future. I cannot imagine how his tenderness could change after he caresses my hair and reassures me *it will all be fine next time. It will be okay, we will be okay, give it time.* "My darling girl, you should have called me. I would have been on the first flight over."

I don't know if this is true but the sentiments are there.

He is sad, he tells me. *It is his loss too. This is new for him as well.* He wraps himself and the duvet around me as the air conditioning is making me shiver. I fall asleep feeling loved, my face pressed against his.

Well the next day it is far from okay as he is sullen and silent and angry with me. He accuses me of causing the miscarriage with my pill popping and drinking and wild behaviour. He is saying it was my fault and he is now angry because it was his child too and I am so reckless and irresponsible. I am not fit to look after myself or anything else. Dancing on tables off my face. I want to say that I wouldn't have been there in the first place losing my mind if he hadn't been so nasty before I went away. He seems to have forgotten this.

This is not helping anyone. It is not helping me get over anything. He tells me I murdered his child as if I had an abortion. As if I ever would. I would never do that. Even if he didn't want the child, I could never do that. I am crying again.

This is nasty. He slaps down breakfast and tells me to eat. *Eat and get some flesh on my goddamn bones. If I wasn't so thin, this might not have happened either. He has to get ready.* My tears drip into my Nutella and toast as he leaves to get changed. "Goddamn child's food," he mutters and ignores me sitting crying into my breakfast.

Tears fall into the plate and when he comes back from the bathroom, he says I should stay at home today, I am too emotional. He says it coldly but then I feel his hands in my hair, his face against mine and he kisses my tears and tells me *he was sorry for being angry, please stay here today and look after yourself and I will bring some nice food home for us.*

"We will get you well again," he says. "I promise. István will take real good care of you."

The next day, he finds a picture I have on my screensaver of me in my underwear and goes mad, demanding I delete it. It is only like someone would appear on the beach. He hates the fact other people may see it. I have left some photos in a file in his apartment of Mariska Hargitay and he even accuses me of wanting her. "I wouldn't say no," I say.

He calls me disgusting. Despite his predatory nature in the bedroom he is very conservative.

This is not normal, he says. *I should not fantasise about beautiful women.* But he obviously prefers this to men. Any hint of me finding a man attractive whether objective or not and he is crazy jealous.

With Mariska's pictures he just tells me, I am not normal. I shouldn't fantasise about this woman.

"Would you say no to her?" I ask him.

"Yes, because of you," he tells me, he can't look up.

"If you want her, it is okay to admit to it," I tell him. She is beautiful, after all.

"I don't want her," he grabs my arms and holds me tightly with both hands, hurting my wrists. "Because I want only you, don't you fucking understand?! Don't you know by now I only want you as long as I fucking live! I can't look at another woman! You kill me when you disappear to another country. You fucking kill me!"

He screams this last part and then slams the door to the bathroom locking himself in for a long time.

I can hear him sobbing broken angry tears despite the running water of the shower.

It breaks my heart.

We are in a fast car to Hell. This is fire which is consuming us both with blistering flames of jealousy which don't stop and won't stop. Until one of us dies, drowning in the other's blood.

One day half-crazy with the central European sun, I run into the dental surgery with a crocodile-skinned avocado pear and shout "Nobody move or I'll pull the pin!"

The receptionists scream and hide under the table as I hurl the avocado across the room.

István goes mad. He comes as close as he can to shaking me until my teeth rattle.

"You see the practice manager about your behaviour, and count this as a verbal warning. What a stupid thing to do."

Fortunately there are no patients around as it is early. It is a stupid thing to do.

The practice manager tells me, *"This isn't a theatre, Kiára and I think you and István need to keep your domestics out of the workplace too. I don't care what's going on outside here, but you are like a bottle of fizzy pop. You need to stop and think that he is your boss in here, whatever goes on elsewhere."*

I tell her I am really sorry. My Sicilian quarter of me can't keep my mouth shut when a man is arguing with me and the Icelandic quarter is always cool but ready to explode like a volcano.

The heat this summer is unbearable. I like the heat, hate the cold but I have been used to the Mediterranean cooling the relentless burn or the more even tempered climate in the Canarias. Central European heat is something else with its landlocked position, there is nowhere for the air to go. I have never been so hot in my life as in southern Hungary where I am literally melting as I walk down the street. The burning Hellfire of the sun doesn't stop, just like our arguments. It is almost worse stepping from the air conditioned dental surgery into the streets which throw me into the volcano. I long to lie in the snow and make angels and feel the cold. Of course, in the winter I will say the opposite. There is no in-between in my world anymore and I miss it.

The next day in work I eat István's chocolate and he goes mad. He's left it on the shelf and it's starting to go white in the sun. He comes into the room as I am stuffing it into my mouth.

"Forgive me, I ate your chocolate heart," I say, my mouth full.

He eyes me and looks at the wrapper on the table.

"Did you ask my permission?" His eyes go darker.

"No, but I was hungry."

"Did you ASK ME?!" he steps closer and puts his hands on my shoulders.

"No, but...."

"You listen to me, baby, you ask me for permission for anything you do. You got that? You got it? Anything." His eyes are now black.

"I'm sorry," I say but I am still laughing.

"And you can have another verbal warning for this." He flounces out of the room. He can't fire me, he hasn't really hired me. Even when it's horrible between us and I ask him does he want me to leave if he hates me so much he looks thoughtful and says "No, I don't want you to leave. I am just angry with you." He can't, or won't let me go.

He grabs my wrist at the end of the day as I have felt-tipped some stars on my wrist while I was thinking what to write on the website.

He drops it in disgust as if I slashed my wrists. "Don't do this in work. It is so like a child."

He always treats me like a child anyway, so what. Big deal, a few drawings which will have washed off by tomorrow. And he said he wanted a child? What is he going to do with this mini-István drawing pictures on his apartment walls? Is he going to treat him or her with the same disgust?

I would probably join in drawing on the wall and István would come and yell at us both and make us repaint the entire apartment as punishment.

No way is he ready. He is a child himself. How can he have one? I have to look after him every night I stay with him but I never bring it up, I never mention the fact I lose sleep taking care of him and his nightmares. I have to get up out of bed as he wanders around the room or the apartment in blind panic in some night terrors, his eyes open in fear. Luckily, he never leaves the apartment and I can lead him back into bed and he will follow and then curl up and fall asleep.

His rages are out of control and he is sexually demanding. He dictates where and when and how. He likes cold hard surfaces when he is feeling angry and he doesn't care if it hurts me. He is still burning

inside about the miscarriage as if my body betrayed
him and he wants to punish me. It is not helping me
get over it. Anyone else would tell me to leave him,
but I am not anyone else and I don't tell anyone else
what is going on. My back is forever bruised from the
shower taps, the sink taps, the kitchen tiles and he is
always sorry afterwards but his moods are up and
down like a yo-yo, he is as bad as me although he uses
his work as a mask; stressful job equates normal up
and down artistic temperament. He doesn't think for
one minute he is remotely like me, apart from in the
looks department where we are clearly evenly
matched. I personally think he is bipolar as I attract
that type and that he should be on Lithium. I wonder
given his fantasies and nightmares about being King
of Hungary that he isn't severe bipolar with psychotic
tendencies which accompany the condition. My shrink
has me on a balance of mood stabilisers,
antidepressants and benzos and István keeps trying
to rip up my prescriptions telling me not to take these
poisonous pills. He demands I hand over the pink
slips of paper and I stuff them into my bra. I stopped
the poisonous contraceptive pill, therefore I should
stop these too. This is his reasoning.

"Give them to me," he says. "You shouldn't be
taking them. What if you get pregnant? It will hurt
the baby. You want that? Don't you care about
nothing but yourself? Maybe they caused the
miscarriage. You stuff your body with poison and
alcohol. You don't eat. What is wrong with you?"

His eyes are black again and he is not used to being
refused.

"No," I tell him. "No, they are mine." I am not
giving up these pills. *Do I live like a saint with no pills
or alcohol just because of what might happen? That is*

insane.

He orders me to cover myself up too. *I show too much flesh. Wear a sweater.*

It's 40c plus and he is telling me to wear a sweater. Added to that I am now working in the kitchen on my computer due to the fact they are worried about tax inspections and I am not on the official payroll. I wear red just to make him madder as he is behaving unreasonably.

I am doing a lot of spells and rituals on his balcony when he's not there, lighting candles and casting circles. I figure he is letting me stay in his huge apartment and this is a big step for him, to trust me like this so I probably should do some lucky love spells. There's a lot of power and energy in southern Hungary. A gypsy woman sees me after a particularly spell-packed weekend while István is on a course in Munich. I chalked a pentagram on the stones of the balcony and set up a real altar of candles. I must remember to clean it up before he is back. I am walking along early in the morning towards the dental surgery when she points at my black rose necklace and asks me what spells I have been doing, she knows I have been doing magic this weekend. I freak out and run down the street and she shouts "Gyere!" *Come back.* The air is thick and dense with a thunderstorm which has been threatening all weekend.

I buy a coffee to take into work when I feel a firm claw on my arm and the same voice asking me what spells I have been doing, she wants to know. I throw my loose coins in her direction and run.

This is too much. I have to stop this black magic. It attracts strange people.

KERESZTRE FESZÍTÉS

One day in the middle of August István drives his car at 140kmph through the city and shooting all the red lights, into the centre of the road up to Tettye, and the sculpture of Christ on a crucifix hangs on the hill like a grim warning in the dying pink light. I ask István *is he trying to kill us?* He laughs and lets go of the wheel and grabs at me. He has done this on the motorway but not on bendy roads in the city. This is a real roll the dice with Death. I think of Lana Del Rey's *Born to Die* video and wonder if this is really what he is doing. We are not wearing seatbelts and if we meet a car on a blind corner, we are all dead or maimed. For some reason we don't meet that car although at 8pm we should by the law of probability and we skid to a halt outside his apartment block, scraping the wall. He is laughing and laughing in a hysterical way. He looks at me to see if I am afraid, like he wanted but I am not. I am not afraid of death as it has already touched me so many times one way or another. An old lady shouts at us from her balcony and calls us crazy; *she is tired of our arguments, our messed up behaviour. What is wrong with us? She wants a quiet life and we are messing it up. This is a good neighbourhood not a gypsy ghetto.*

Her chocolate labrador is barking and growling. We don't answer her. I am about to give her the finger but István grabs my hands in his lightning response and twists them behind my back as he marches me into the apartment and shoves me into the wall when we are inside, ripping my clothes off. Neither of us mentions this incident again but despite his protests of love of living, I have thought that he is half-crazy too and suffers the same mood swings as me but hides it underneath a ton of work. We sit on the sofa for a minute in silence and outside, the tyres are still burning. I wonder why we didn't die. I wonder why he wanted us to die together. He is clearly exhilarated by this near death ride as he half-sighs with happiness and almost seems disappointed that we are still sitting together alive. Why doesn't he just strangle us both? I am not afraid. He is still in a strange manic state for the rest of the evening and night. It has made him feel extremely aroused, this car crash fantasy. He ties my wrists to the bed; his prisoner. We share an ecstasy as though it is our last night on earth which lasts until sunrise.

He kisses the scar on my jawbone and tells me *I am his, I am his possession and he can do what he wants to me.* But he is gentle. His body contradicts his angry words and actions. I fall asleep next to him with his delicate fingers stroking my spine.

"Sweet passionate girl," he whispers. "My love, my life, my everything."

Early next morning, he is up and in the shower and I know even before I see him his mood will have flipped over. Neither of us slept very much. When he gets up without touching me I know he is angry and trying to push me away in his own head. He hates the fact that he lost control.

He is leaving for Italy and a load of conferences later that day. The personality switch snaps and he is cold and tells me he will be away for three weeks and he doesn't want me in his apartment while he is gone. He probably saw remnants of my magic spells; the wax, the candles and the ghost of the pentagram which is still there despite me scrubbing away at the balcony to try to remove it.

I tell him fine, go to who he is going to in Italy, I hope she makes him happy.

He tells me to *shut the hell up; this is work not a fuckfest.*

How would I know? I say.

I stopped taking my contraceptive pill in May so I feel like I am already playing Russian roulette with my life.

He knows this and he likes it. He likes the fact we are playing with fire. He says it makes him feel more excited, he secretly is hoping for a happy accident only this morning he is anything but excited and kind.

He is angry with me. *Extremely angry* he says that final morning before he leaves for Italy. He tells me, *I am not giving him his heir to the throne. What is wrong with me? Am I as infertile as an orange tree in Norway? Or am I just a selfish woman who drinks and parties and destroys any living being inside her like I did the last time?*

"You what?" I say, thinking I have misheard him. But he is looking at me with cold angry eyes.

"Fine, go to Italy and you will soon get an heir to your fucking throne!" I shout, and swallow the last of my coffee. "Feel free to fuck the whole of Italy for all I care! I hope next year there are a thousand Istváns in Italy, then you will be happy, István a Király!"

What a fruitcake. Heir to the throne. Who does he think he is?

His eyes are so cold and dead and without feeling that he is the polar opposite of how he was last night. I say I have plenty of people to see and I move into my friend's travellers' hostel, left to make sense of it all, wishing we had died together in the car crash on one level, angry that he doesn't just talk about his feelings on the other, but he's a Hungarian man, a knight from the middle ages, why would he admit to feeling anything. The heat rises and it reaches 44c in southern Hungary and I climb into the ornate fountain by the theatre with all my clothes on. There's some law I think where it's legal to get into the water after it reaches 40c outside. I am frenzied, waking at 4.30am full of useless ideas, half-working, half-wasting the extra time I have. I meet a range of messed up characters. I have dinner with a different one each night and it all ends the same way. I have a magnet in my heart for trouble. They seem mesmerised by my theatrical nature and I meet more bipolars than I care to think about. What is it with this illness, is there some kind of bipolar radar?

I can't sleep in bed, it's too hot and I wake up in oppressive heat, no air conditioning or fan so I take my sheet and cocoon myself in it on the sofa. I am having nightmares and waking up shouting. *I keep wishing we had died together in the car that night. Maybe that's the only way we can be together as our relationship is so full of fire and angst. Maybe we just need to burn to death entwined and melt our flesh into one.*

I travel up to Budapest to see my shrink. The air conditioning breaks down 10 minutes into the journey and everyone sits in the oven, unable to open windows. When I step off the train in Déli station, the 40c heat seems cool in comparison. This is the day I get caught riding the trams with the same ticket I've had for a long time. The inspector turns round and I try to validate the ticket but he rips it out of my hands and shouts at me in Hungarian. I've had this planned for a while so I shout back in Spanish

'No entendio. No hablo inglés, no hablo hungaro.'

We are stuck at the red lights at Moszkva Tér for

an eternity while this insane dialogue goes on, him trying English and German and telling me all the while I must pay the fine, he will call the police. I keep shouting in Spanish while the whole tram carriage looks on. Finally when we reach the next stop I leap out and run. He yells after me in Hungarian "You're Hungarian and you know what you're doing!"

I do know what I'm doing but then half of Budapest are riding around and jumping off when the inspectors get on but money is so tight right now with István away and I'm not being paid as it's August national holiday, ironically for Szent István a Király only his reincarnation is not here but brooding alone in Italy without me. I should call him on August 20th and wish him happy king's day but I know it would be nasty of me.

I decide to visit Osijek in Croatia as it is near the Hungarian border. I stay in a strange hostel and no one speaks a word of English or Hungarian. I can't understand them, they can't understand me. I feel like the town is in a time trap. I am melting in the heat. It must be past 44c now and I am walking up the road from the train station in the midday sun. I must be crazy. I watch the news in the hostel and understand one word in 3 hours; *temperatura.*

It is after the car incident that August that I decide István really is dangerous and I am going to Sicily. I will never come back. He senses this which is why he tried to kill us both. I can accept madness but not his hot and cold, fire and ice where he pulls me towards him and then pushes me away again. It is messing with my head. I have told him it is only a week's holiday but he knows my pattern by now. Disappear somewhere across Europe. Flying into Sicily I see the volcanic island that reminds me of the Canaries and feel maybe this will be my chance to get away from István for good.

He has called me from Italy while he was away and gone crazy that I spoke to his colleague about some work. He tells me I deal with him and no one else. He is jealous of this handsome young dentist, Gábor who is sweet and always kind. I like Gábor but he is handsome in a kind wholesome way and I know there are no hidden secrets with him. I know he would probably drive me insane with his trusting nature. I almost need these dangerous men to feel alive. In all the other phone calls István makes to me he is abrupt and rude; he orders me to stay away from Gábor and tells me he will find out if I have fucked him. He is not having another man's child around him, I will get out and go as far away as I can if it comes to that. He will test the DNA a thousand times to make sure any kid I have is his and not another man's. *He will hunt down all the evidence,* he snarls down the phone. *He will install cameras in every room in the dental surgery if he has to.*

I tell him *to stop being so crazy, doesn't he want me to be civil to his staff?*

Fuck you, he says as he hangs up.

His self-imposed exile from me is making him more rabidly jealous than ever. He did it as he feels like he is in control, he refused my offer to go over there to see him for a week, after all I speak Italian. It has only proved he can't deal with his emotions at all.

No, he has said. *You are not my goddamn wife. Stop trying to control me. You don't get to decide if you come to Italy, sweetheart. Stay away from me, I need my space.*

You can have it, I say. *I will never bother you again. I am going to Sicily which is full of beautiful men.*

Find your own fucking heir to your throne.

He slams down the phone.

I start to think that I really don't care if he is fucking some Italian while he is away. I can't understand just why he has to be so unpleasant when we could have a nice life together. I just want him to get in or get out but he seems unable to do either. I hear from other people that all his romances are short-lived or non-existent. People warn me he only lives for work. He has never been married and they think he never will be. I feel that this is the end of us, burning in rage and passion and jealousy, a bonfire of angry painful emotions.

Once I am in Sicily and feel I have shaken off the shackles of István, I am working in Palermo but it is not peachy. I am horribly allergic to the mosquitoes which gather outside my window in a dirty water tank and my legs are covered in their bites which look like purple bruises. I am afraid of the chaotic traffic, the scooters, the noise and I trip all the time on broken paving slabs. Every day there's a protest against something or other. The only thing I like are the sweet breakfasts with fresh juice, sugar dusted cornets of cream and café latte. *I miss István so much it hurts. I have not shaken him off. I feel like I have cut out my heart and left it in his apartment. It belongs to him.*

I keep getting texts from Hungary which hurt:

I was wrong about you. You are not my Queen. She would never behave like you. She would be here with me.

Once I get one which nearly makes me pack up and go back. ***Kiára, I will come and get you if you do not come back to me. I am dying without you. I am dying, baby.***

I don't reply and then I realise I have used up a lot of credit on my phone when I am eating breakfast and I must have called István at midnight or later, half-drunk and angry and we must have been shouting for 20 minutes at a time. I just never remember. I am so stressed and eating so little that I am forgetting everything when I have a drink.

One text from him just says: **Utálak. Utálak. Utálak.** *I hate you, I hate you, I hate you.*

Sicily is a closed island, so different from the Italy I know. It is like Corsica in many ways.

I am so unhappy I have an affair with my boss mainly in the Lavanderia in the building. I know it is suicidal, I don't even like him that much and he always thanks me after sex. "Grazie, grazie, Kiára."

I tell him this is not necessary but he says he does it as he is a gentleman.

Yes, and I am a fallen angel you cheating Sicilian mafia man. I usually close my eyes and think of István although I feel no guilt for cheating on him, or for cheating with this married man.

After 2 weeks his wife confronts me and throws my Italian dictionary at my head shouting,

"Strega, strega, vai, vai!" She has found the time to go into my room and search my suitcases and takes the Italian obscenities to mean I am having an affair with her husband. Which I might not have been. I write Italian obscenities anyway or anything which may be useful in a new country.

They throw me and my suitcases out on the streets.

I head to Catania and pick up a bit of work. The city seems nice until you take one step out of the Duomo square and fall over the piles of rotting rubbish in the streets, the short Sicilian men smoking away as there is no work. Catania is depressed and poverty-stricken. Even in Duomo square, the carabinieri are on constant watch and like Palermo, there's a protest every day. I cry in the delicatessen, the bag shop, the cake shop and just mention the word 'amore' and the Sicilians understand and give me a discount on everything for my pain.

My Spanish and Italian languages have fused to make an insane language of its own. Even a South American I meet has trouble separating the two tongues so when I leave I give him my Spanish/Italian dictionary. He is also bipolar and tells me his father strangled his mother and then shot himself. This is the second man I've met who this has happened to. Just like the Canary Islands, everyone is running away from something or other.

I hate the haggling over money which is so alien in Eastern Europe. I take pity on a flower seller in the bus station and buy two red roses for three euros but he looks bad-tempered and tries to sell me more. No, I tell him.

Sto morendo de fame, he tells me. He is clearly not dying of hunger as he says and I tell him this to his fat stomach and that I eat on three euros a day so why can't he.

He stomps off muttering.

Fucking hagglers, I think.

The September sun hardly penetrates the dark narrow streets where strings of washing hang from window to window. I work for three weeks, see Taormina and Enna and think this is enough. Taormina is full of mafia and Enna is full of strange Romanians. I call István in work and tell him I am coming back the next day. "Good," he says. "Good. I knew if I didn't call you that you would return. You are returning to me, my lady."

He is triumphant as he has won. He didn't need to come and get me. I am doing it myself. The bonfire burns on, glowing red embers. It will burn for a long time to come.

I leave Catania early on a dark October morning to get my flight back to Budapest. I can't take it here anymore. But the 3 metre iron gates at the front of the apartment block are locked. If I had any sense I would see the glowing switch on the side to release the lock.

But I have no sense, otherwise I wouldn't be here in the first place. I shout "Aiuto, soccorso!" to some men passing my iron prison but they ignore me. They don't want to help me and my suitcases over the gate at 5am. So I climb as high as I can and hurl the cases over and manage to scramble up a bit of wall in my high heels, my dress round my waist. I have no underwear and I am too desperate to be embarrassed. I hang as low as I can over the iron gates and drop, scraping up the whole of my right arm.

By the afternoon I am back in the dental surgery and István accuses me of self-harming when he sees the bleeding scrapes on my arm. He doesn't buy my story about being locked in but for once it's true. He just sprays the cuts with antiseptic and tells me I have to stop doing this to myself, for one thing it's bad for business. I am propelled back to Hungary no matter how hard I try to stay away. I am either very careless or this is fate. He reluctantly lets me stay in his apartment although I can see he isn't happy. This makes me sad as despite all the pain and violent mood swings, I have realised I love him more than I could ever say and would accept him and his faults whatever. I can't see it isn't because he doesn't love me but because he does and so much and so obsessively, he does not know what to do with all this love he is feeling. This is why he is reluctant to let me in. He is afraid of getting closer and then I announce I am off again. He tells me *I have hurt his heart, I am a bad girl. His heart is damaged and it is all my fault*, he says.

He grills me about what and who I was doing in Sicily and even tells me to go and have myself tested for STDs. I tell him why doesn't he do the same? He says he doesn't need to as he is tested for Hepatitis B and HIV for his dental licence. I say he could still have the clap. I clap my hands and laugh.

"It isn't funny," he tells me. "I am a pure man."

In the end we both go to get tested, me for the whole range and him for half. Just to prove the other wrong.

We sit side by side hating each other, each so mistrustful. I know I cheated but I was safe. I feel guilty for cheating as I don't think he would cheat. Whatever his flaws, he is not a cheater. I cheat as I think it is inadvertently hurting him but I feel horrible afterwards when it is him I wanted and not the guy I cheated with, like the Sicilian man.

Of course the STD results are clear for both of us.

He tells me, *I am a distraction, he can't sleep with me in his bed as he needs my body like a drug*. He says this every night and still needs his fix and then is moody and sullen in the morning. Sometimes he orders me to go and sleep in one of his spare rooms as he says he will never sleep if I am with him but I always creep back into his bed when he is asleep around 3am and lie as still as I can until I fall asleep myself and wake to find him angry and aroused. He tells me *I am a bad, bad girl. He had no distractions before he met me and now I am depriving him of his sleep.*

I tell him *he doesn't have to spend hours feasting on my flesh, as that is what he does. He could always sleep much earlier.* I ask him *what does he think he is going to do if he has a kid screaming all night, every night?*

He says *this is different and anyway, I would have to deal with him or her. He is the one who needs his sleep.*

Yeah, I say. *I thought that would be true. What if I am not around, what if you are alone?*

Then I would deal with it, he says arrogantly.

I don't need to self-harm. His bites do that for me. Vampire. And his cruel words.

One of the dental assistants sees my back as I am taking my sweater off one day and gasps in horror.

"Did he do that to you?"

"What?" I have already forgotten as it is so common now, this vampire man.

"Look in the mirror," she says.

I step into the bathroom and she is right to comment. My back is covered in red and purple bites.

She tells me *he is hurting me, he is cruel and I don't have to put up with this.*

I tell her *I am fine.* I don't want to add; *But I like it.*

She will think I am crazy. I just tell Gabi *not to say anything to the others, please.*

She agrees.

HÁNYTŰZ TÉL

UTÁL

I'm burned down to the bone
It will take more than skin grafts
To repair the damage you have done
Every pulse of racing red fluid
Through my body
Brings its own sharp stab of misery
and then repeats with a murderous intensity as
it flows back to its source

Slower, darker, thicker and throbbing
the colour of a potent Egri Bikavér

An endless cycle of pain

It never fades
It never stops
I will never forget you

Summer has hung on with its claws into October and like me, it can hold on no longer. We slide off the precipice together towards the jagged rocks below. It's 10th October and the sun is dying. It starts to cool and I am in deadlock with István. I am feeling guilty about the cheating I did in Sicily even though this is my way of hurting him without him knowing.

Only I know, and I feel worse. I am just hurting myself and my heart.

I feel so bad cheating on István with the Sicilian and I feel so horrible treating him like dirt at times. Telling him, *why would I want to be with him for the rest of my life?*

It is as though I want to hurt him for all the pain he has caused me. I bottle it up and save it for when he is at his weakest and then spit the poison cobra-like into his face.

He is crushed when I say things like this and one night I am so nasty with my tongue lashing he crumples into a ball in the corner of the bedroom and stays that way for hours. Catatonic. I have brought him to this, curled up like a child.

This is not love, this is obsession and sickness and sado-masochism and we both do it, we are both guilty and it will never cease.

I hate myself and I am pleading with him after moments like this. I am telling him, *I love him so much my heart could die. I want him and I will be with him forever if he wants me.* I mean it.

He thinks I don't.

He never says the word love to me.

I can't face November. Day of the Dead is gloomy, the polar opposite to its Mexican counterpart, where I once danced with orange flowers in my hair in the sunshine. In Hungary, the sky is grey, the cemeteries are grey and the trees are dying. I stay in bed all day. At the end of November we have a huge argument and he tells me *I am not his goddamn wife, he doesn't want a nagging wife.*

I scream at him "No wonder you've never been married. You are just a horrible man underneath your good looks and money. You are nothing to me, nothing. You are not the King of Hungary!"

"Get out of my apartment," he tells me. "Just get the hell out and leave me to my work. I was fine before I met you."

"Sure you were, you were so starved of affection,

you didn't even know what to do with it," I say.

I take my laptop and tell him I'm going to work on the websites and my column I still write for the Russian newspaper from Tenerife. I've got writer's block in this gloom. It angers him that I write and speak Russian especially that I still work for a Russian publication. He like many Hungarians over the age of forty sees it as a hateful language of oppression. One day I call back at his apartment to get something and I find him burning my Russian dictionary and some novels. I fly into a rage and leap at him like a wild cat but he catches both my wrists and keeps me at arm's length. I am mad. He laughs in my face. At times I hate him so much my heart feels like it will explode. We have this pointless argument every now and then.

How many times do I have to explain I studied Russian at university, I didn't grow up in Hungary, I didn't know of the horrors that went on until I was much older.

I am still angry with him for trying to kill us in August and then telling me deadpan that I couldn't stay in his apartment while he was away. I am angry he hardly called while he was away and when he did he had nothing to say. I want to hurt him but I don't even know if he is capable of feelings. He has changed his phone number and told me, *I am not to have it; I am not a good girl, I am not a nice girl.*

He looks at me wanting me to beg for his number.

I don't. I tell him, *he never answers and he has nothing interesting to say anyway. He is a boring man and he will die alone. His head is full of fucking teeth and scalpels and surgery,* I say.

I am sick of you treating me like a second class citizen, when I am smarter than you and I can have any man I want. Get over yourself, you're a middle aged dentist and surgeon in Hungary not a rock star. And you are alone. And seriously, do you really think you are fit to have a kid, which is what is going to happen to us given the way you don't take any responsibility?

This cuts into him visibly as he crumples in the doorway, hate and pain in his face. He hates the fact I referred to his age and he tells me, *he would be a good parent, it is me who is the problem. If I hate him that much,* he says, *I can have his baby and leave it with him and he will look after it while I am tarting my way across Europe. He can do my parenting for me and he doesn't need me around.*

In fact he only wants a beautiful child and that is the only reason to be with me. I would give him the beautiful baby he deserves.

Yes, that is the answer. He stands up tall and tells me so.

"Let me give you a baby and then you can just leave it with me and go and do whatever you want with whoever you want. You are beautiful, Kiára, but you are a fuck up! I want your lovely child but I don't want you! That's the first thing I thought of when I met you. I don't want another woman but I want a child and then you can just leave. I am mature enough to care for him or her without you."

"Bastard!" I shout. I shove him hard and walk out. He has cut me to pieces.

He slams the apartment door.

As I am walking away burning with anger, my chest is stabbing and my stomach is eating away at itself. I look back and he is on his balcony watching me go. I turn back again further down the street and he is still there motionless in the darkness, his black hair wild in the night wind and the cold cuts through me as I realise the tears are falling down my face.

"Kiára, please come back to me, I am sorry.... I need you. Please, I didn't mean to say what I did......" he calls through the night sky. A jagged sliver of crescent moon grins down at me.

I keep walking.

I think this is the last I will see of him. We have been nastier this time than usual. It hurts me to hurt him but then he always hurts me first or is it the other way round, I don't even know anymore.

I never see an argument as just an argument, I always believe the things people say and I believe this so much that he has seen me from Day One and thought he wanted a child and here is someone who will give him what he wants and then he can get rid of her afterwards and bring up the child as his own, with me kicked out.

He wants a beautiful replica of himself. He is so messed up.

But no, the day I am due to fly he calls me from a private number. He has to travel to Budapest that day for a conference so he takes me to the airport. It's a nice gesture. But I am still burning with the pain he caused the other night and every question, which is tentative and not accusatory from him I just don't answer.

He then doesn't say anything until I am getting out of the car.

Then I hear "I don't want you to go. Why do you keep doing this to me? Why do you hurt me like this?"

"Why didn't you say that yesterday or last week, or last month?" I ask. I am half in and half out of the car. "Why don't you talk to me? Why do you always just close me out and throw me out of your apartment and take away your phone number?"

"I want you to have it if you are a good girl," he says. "You are not a good girl."

His eyes are staring straight ahead, his lovely lips tight shut with anger or pain and he is gripping the steering wheel.

I am a good girl, I tell him *and he is breaking my heart. Didn't he remember what he said to me about he only wanted a child and not me?*

He says, *he was so sorry. He cried all night after we had that argument. He cried because he said everything to hurt me and none of it was true. Of course he wants me. He wants me all the time, good or bad Kiára. Cruel or kind. He wants me forever. I belong with him.*

He sounds genuine but I can't imagine him crying all night, or crying at all. He might just be saying all this now.

He slaps my ass hard as I am hanging over the seat to get my suitcase and says "You're a bad girl for doing this to me, for hurting me like this. No one ever did this to me before, no one."

Then he kisses me so hard I taste blood. He tugs my hair so roughly, some of it tears away. Candy floss girl. It is still dark outside this being a really early flight and I can't help myself, he can't help himself and he pushes up my dress and we fuck in the car and some more and more still until it is getting close to my check in time and I hope no one sees us. I can't let go and he can't let go; he is holding my face to his so tight, but I have to in the end or I will miss my flight. It is horrible to tear myself away from the smell of his skin, his hair. I am tearing my own heart out and leaving it on the dashboard.

"You hurt me," he says afterwards. "You always

hurt me, and you're not wearing any underwear, you slut." His eyes are wounded. "Leaving me like this in the cold and the dark."

"Worked for you didn't it, this morning?" I say pulling my dress back into shape. It's easier to travel like this, doesn't mean I am going to fuck my way around the Canary Islands.

I didn't even think he was capable of hurting. I've always pictured his heart like a Siberian prison; frozen solid and surrounded with deathly razor wire. Impenetrable and only capable of cutting anyone who tried to get in there to pieces. I don't realise that if anyone is already in there, they will never get out again. They will never make it over the razor wire alive. The only escape is death via the prison cemetery where they can never truly be free. I don't know this yet. I just think my problem is the getting into the prison.

He has his head in his hands slumped over the steering wheel twisting my hair he has just wrenched out through his fingers.

"Talk to me," I say. But he won't. He has snapped shut.

"Just go," he says shakily, not looking up. I am worried for the first time in history he is about to cry in front of me. I touch his arm gently. "István....."

"Get away from me." Without looking up he pushes me away from him hard.

"Please," I say to him.

"Get out, just get out."

He would hate me to see him weak. I try to take his hand but he pulls it away and tells me, *go, get out. Just get the hell out and go to whoever it is I am going to, however many there are.* There are tears in his voice but he is burying his head in his hands.

I promise to come back. I tell him, *I am not going to anyone. There is no man in Spain.*

I look back as I am about to go into the departures terminal and he is still in the same position in his car. He is crying, I am sure and I want to run back and forget this stupid flight. I fight every fibre in my body which is screaming for me to turn around and run back to him and tell him I love him more than anything, more than I can ever say, however good or bad or crazy it is. I would be happy in fucking Norilsk with him.

We are both so fucked up how is this ever going to work?

The plane touches down in Tenerife and I inhale the air in the warm evening. I love the scent of these islands. The moon is smiling at me like a melon slice low and large. I am staying in an old Canarian house in La Orotava with friends and a constant stream of travellers and backpackers. It doesn't take long before I am manic in the sun. I write early in the morning when it's still dark as I know each day will end up the same way; dancing on the roof terrace with a bottle of wine and gazing at the stars, high on volcanic energy. Some days I spend on the black sand beaches gazing up at Mount Teide which looks like Mount Fuji with its snow cap. I love the cemeteries with their dazzling white walls and red and orange flowers, the dead encased in the stone as digging into the volcanic soil would be futile.

I am desperate to swim but the Atlantic is too ferocious so I head to Lago Martianez in Puerto de la Cruz with Adam, an Australian who is drinking his way round Europe. The water is freezing and after 5 minutes my body is white with cold and I can't stop shivering for an hour despite the 28c temperature outside. The house we are in is haunted to Hell and back. Every night at 3am exactly I wake up to the door in the corner of my room shaking violently. It's locked and something in there is trying to get out. The landlord laughs and says it's only the breeze but there is no breeze. A series of travellers spend one or two nights in the room near mine and I ask them how they slept the next morning as we eat breakfast. The answers are what I am expecting "I can't spend another night in this haunted house, there was something IN my room, I tell you."

So it's not just me.

It is freaking me out so I light some candles to send the ghost to its afterlife and leave a tray of milk and biscuits. That night I wake up at 3am and I hear rustling in the corner of the room instead of the violent shaking. The tee light I set out nearest the door burns all night. It's still burning in the morning. I don't see how this is possible but the paranormal activity stops after this.

I always wondered if these volcanic islands led to strange occurrences. One day a young traveller appears to spend a night in the haunted house as he is travelling around the islands. He smiles and I think he looks familiar. He says he is Sam from Tajikistan and he has a message for me. I show him pictures of István. He studies them carefully. He tells me never to discuss my love with anyone. Never. They will only try to destroy it. He's right as when I have told people about him they always say "Forget this Hungarian dentist, he sounds crazy, dangerous and just work-obsessed. You're wasting your time."

The next morning I am sitting on the seafront with Sam and he tells me he once drove from Tajikistan to London for love. He was going out of his mind. Then all at once there is a chill in the warm air, the blue sky seems to darken and Sam's broad smile fades and he says to me "And now my work here is done. I have to go now. Don't forget what I told you."

He walks away and I wonder if we all haven't just been drinking too much cheap duty-free wine every night or if these meetings really happen.

I sit on the roof terrace that night and watch the melon moon rise, a split mouth which is glowing a sinister shade of red. It rises up from the ocean and gives me a Hallowe'en pumpkin leer before slowly sliding back into the water. It reminds me of midsummer in Sweden when the sun appears to set, a glowing red fireball at midnight and then seems to change its mind and rises up again.

It is 1st December and I get a call from István. I am lying in the sun on the rooftop talking to some Danish travellers. We are all escaping our miserable winters.

He is going to Norway for a conference. He thinks this might also be a chance to get some Scandinavian business for his dental surgery. He expects me to meet him there.

Why? You don't even like me, I say.

He is silent, all those 4,000 km away. I wonder if I lost the phone connection.

"No I don't," he says. "I don't like you but I expect you there. I already booked your ticket to Oslo for 8th December. Check your emails and print your boarding pass. You work for me and I need you there that week, you told me your relatives are Scandinavian."

"Whatever," I say.

"And I don't like you. I really hate you, you slut."

"I hate you as well, you are a cruel man, a jealous nasty man," I say feeling pain from all this distance as though he is right there next to me.

"But I love you too and I need you. I love you, Kiára. I've always loved you."

I want to speak but the words are frozen on my tongue and then the phone line goes dead. He has hung up.

I can't believe this last remark. It stretches across the Atlantic from where I am standing on the roof terrace in the white sunlight and rebounds around me all the way with magnetic force from the frozen dark heart of the man in cold dark Hungary. The man who never loves, who never lets anyone in and yet just told me he loves me.

I have to sit down.

Infinity.

My heart is racing.

I watch a perfect rainbow form over the Atlantic in the north and its end spills into a white church. I don't see how this can happen. It is not even raining. It shimmers there in the direction of Hungary.

I decide this is a sign. I go downstairs and open my email. Sure enough there is a ticket booked for me via Madrid to Oslo for 8th December. I want him so much it hurts.

NORVÉGIA

You find me in Oslo
In the soft plum-coloured dark December
I'm installed in the *Munch Museet*
Where I've spent the last hour
Worshipping *The Scream*
My memento to misery
I love it

You take me to the white bright lights
Inside the hotel
We eat reindeer stir fry and moose pie
And chase it with frosty shots of vodka
Then you fly me north
Slicing over the Arctic Highway
To *Tromsø*
And its ghostly green curtains
Which give me a nightly performance
Above the glittering city

Maybe I should be more careful
We nearly hit an elk on the road
In this Paris of the North
I see its red eyes shining in the headlamps
And the taxi driver swerves and curses
A warning

I don't really know you
And your frozen heart

But I have to trust you

My flight is some hours before István's so I take this

opportunity to go to the Munch museum. I have never seen **Skrik** or *The Scream*. I spend so long in the museum dazzled by all the paintings which chart the Norwegian artist's descent into depression and then back up again. I text István to let him know where I am.

I feel a hand on my shoulder and I am wrenched out of my daydream. It is István. He is in brown Armani and his eyes are soft and full of tenderness. He is so beautiful. I keep making my mind up that I will be strong and that all gets shot to Hell when I see him. Especially when he is in a good mood and the lightness shows in his smile and he looks at me like I am an angel fallen from Heaven. At times like this I feel I never saw a more beautiful man in my life and I understand how he feels when he says, *he wants to drink me in and devour my flesh*. I have the same urge.

"I thought I would come and find you here, I wanted to see *The Scream* too."

But he doesn't even like art, I think. He looks at it for a minute, says this place is depressing and we should go to the hotel, we need to prepare for tomorrow's conference. I know he doesn't understand Munch but I feel the artist's paintings as if he is speaking into my ear, painting my body with his palette and spinning me in a dizzy circle through his life. I can feel the colours in three dimension, a synaesthesia of crying blue, screaming red and insanity yellow.

Reindeer meat is just dull and I can't chew it anyway so I order the moose pie. It's just like any I have eaten in Sweden or Norway before and just as overpriced. This is all so touristy, I think. István doesn't approve of my shots of vodka especially as I don't really enjoy them. I just like the novelty of them being served in tiny glasses made of ice which gives my lips freezer burn. He is drinking just the one glass of white wine.

"Slow down, baby. I need you to be fresh for tomorrow," he says with anger after my third frosty shot. It burns going down.

Okay. I throw the ice glass over my shoulder since our table is by the wall and it shatters. I like this, he tells me to stop being such a child.

We are in the elevator going up to the top floor. I see him looking at me in the mirror. He has that blank dead look where I wonder where he is. His spirit seems to have gone and he is just a body. How can a person change so quickly? With him I can never blame drink. He drinks a little, but just with dinner. He isn't a drinker and his moods change with or without alcohol. In the time I have known him he has only ever had a maximum of half a bottle of wine over dinner, never more. I am glad he isn't a drinker but his mood swings which have no pattern or reason disturb me.

"What's wrong?" I ask him.

He doesn't speak, just shoves me against the wall hard and tears my dress in half with one hand.

He pushes himself against me.

"No, István," I say. "Not here."

"What's the matter? Don't like it rough, do you? Bet you had it rough all your life and now you're a goddamn princess..."

"Stop it," I tell him. "Just wait until we are in the room."

He remembers himself and steps back "I am sorry," he says. "I'm really sorry."

"Anyway you always call me your Queen, King

István of Hungary," I say and laugh.

He looks at the floor, ashamed. He is split down the centre; reserved and a gentleman on one side and underneath it all, the other side is a complete raging animal. He is mortified that I made reference to his secret fantasy or reality. I actually don't know what it is. It is real enough in the middle of the night to him.

He is silent as he unlocks the door and I feel bad for mentioning his fantasy or fucked up reality.

The stark white bathroom has a clinical feel. He likes this. He drags me away from the nice soft bedroom, plush purple and cream with a velvety bedspread and into the operating theatre. I am still holding a pillow, he is so fast. I am tired after the two plane rides and want to lie down in this plump coloured softness. No, he wants the hard white wall and bright bathroom lights. He throws the pillow back into the soft bedroom and pushes me against the bathroom tiles.

I tell him, *to wait as I have stopped taking my contraceptive pill back in May and I have played Russian roulette since then and so has he and right now is the middle of the month, I can't deal with worrying again. It is only a matter of time before my luck runs out. My body is not healthy to give life to anything that tries to live inside it either.*

He says, *so what, it isn't healthy to take the pill anyway.* He is not worried about the consequences. He keeps on and on about his heir to the throne and I don't need to do anything apart from give him what he wants and leave. I tell him I have condoms in my bag but he says, *they are only for sluts and he doesn't like them.*

If I am faithful to him why would I need them? He says *it offends him I brought them.*

I tell him I was so worried last time my time of the month was late.

"You don't have to worry if it happens, it is good," he says without any emotion whatsoever.

"It is what I want and what you need. But I don't expect you to stay, Kiára. You are not the maternal kind."

He is cruel. *I hate him. I love him. I hate him. I........*

He doesn't even take off his suit. He is not taking no for an answer. He doesn't remember our last argument only a couple of weeks' ago. I know he desperately wants a baby. He knows when I am at my most fertile, only I personally think I am still too thin for it to happen but it drives him on all the same. He thinks he is man enough, he has said it enough times.

"There," he says when he is done. "Isn't that better?"

It is more of a statement than a question as he goes to wash his face in the sink without looking at me. He sounds as if he just performed some kind of surgery and now he is scrubbing up for the next patient.

"István," I say with my eyes closed and slide to the floor dizzy. My body is addicted to him.

I feel like a takeaway dinner. I am the takeaway. I go back into the soft bedroom and throw my dress in the garbage. He has torn it so much he had better buy me a new one. I look out of the window at the glittering white lights across Oslo.

He calls me from the bathroom. "Baby, come and join me in the shower."

I don't answer. I have had enough for today. I just want to get into that bed.

I start to climb into the velvety heaven.

But it is not an invitation, it's an order as he comes

to get me again.

"I'll buy you a new dress, darling," he says as he pulls me into the shower. "Anything you want I buy for you, just make me happy tonight, be a good girl. I told you I need you here this week."

"I am a good girl," I say under the rainhead shower.

"You are not," he says as he pins me against the wall. "You left me alone and hurt me, no one does that to me. You are a bad, bad girl."

I like the hurt of the hot water and him hurting me and the cold hard tiles. I want to hurt. And some more. I feel the bruises coming up already. I shouldn't like it but I do, feeling him biting me and tasting my blood in his kisses.

I am a total masochist. God help the kid if it turned out like us.

A few days later we have to be in the north of Norway. I wanted to drive up to the north but it would take too long so we take a flight up to Tromsø. I like it, as it is unique but István is tired having tried to cram too much into the week, taking in Oslo and up to the frozen north where neither of us has brought the right clothes so we can't leave the hotel unless it is straight in a taxi to the conference. One evening I am looking out over the winter wonderland and I see the northern lights. Like some strange phosphorescent green curtain from heaven, twisting and turning. It is so magical and I shout to István who is lying on the bed, *to come and look, it's the northern lights and it looks like the elves are having a party in the sky.*

He doesn't answer. He hasn't said much all day. I go over to him and he is lying there staring at the wall. I ask him is he feeling okay. He closes his eyes and shakes his head. He won't open his eyes.

"Honey, are you sick?" I ask.

He won't answer me. He is just curled up in a ball unable to move. I wonder if the darkness of Norway has got to him. I stroke his hair. The curls are soft and silky.

His forehead is not warm but he won't say what is wrong. He won't open his eyes. I don't know what to do. It isn't like him. *Would he like something hot to drink?*

No answer. He isn't there. Only his body is there curled up tight.

I just sit there and stroke his hair and tell him it's okay, I'm here.

A tear slides from under his eyelashes and wets my fingers.

"I love you, I love you so much," I tell him.

He doesn't move or speak and I just hope it reaches him whichever dark place he is in.

"István, you are my life. Let me take care of you," I tell him. "I am sorry for all the bad words I said, please forgive me if I ever hurt you."

I can't go to sleep, I have to watch over him. He has nightmares and is shouting "Nem, nem!" and wrestling with demons and the bedsheets. He is the King of Hungary again and maybe tonight he is fighting with the Vikings.

I tell him *it's okay, I am here, the light is on. I won't leave him*. He grabs hold of me and holds me like I am a child's teddy bear.

"Anya," he says. "Anya." Mother.

His face is damp with sweat, his black curls sticking to his forehead and he is gasping for air. He is so afraid and I don't know why he is having these night terrors and what they are about.

I know he is sick and I wish he would tell me and I could take care of him. I would give up my life for him.

I finally fall asleep at 5am as I am so tired. I wake up and he is out of bed and in the shower, the clock says 7am but it is as dark as midnight all the time here, the sky just turning a little plum-tinted around lunchtime, but it is permanent Arctic darkness this far north in Norway. I go to the bathroom to clean my teeth and ask him, *is he okay, is he feeling better now?*

"What the hell are you talking about?" he snaps as he grabs the towel out of my hands. "Leave me alone, will you?"

He glares at me in my lingerie under the bright bathroom strip light as I clean my teeth and without a word lifts me on to the sink. My back hurts pressed into the taps and he closes his eyes in happiness and ecstasy. Operating theatre mood lighting and he is happy. He says, *he feels so satisfied now. I am a good girl. I am pleasing him very much this week.*

I am left worrying about my contraceptive pills thousands of kilometres away from this situation and now useless. I should have started taking it again and not told him. What the Hell is he thinking of taking chances like this? He is trying to take chances to bind him to me forever. Someone he loves and hates at the same time.

I have visions of my body trying to fight him off deep inside my uterus and failing. He is strong and healthy and I will lose.

He kisses me long and deep and pulls my hair and holds me against him. He is in Heaven. The sink taps bite into my back.

However, he is moody all day and won't speak to me in the conference.

We stay another night in the frozen city and it is the same experience. Reindeer meat and moose pie, frozen vodka in ice glasses and him moody and strange and when I want to climb into the perfectly made bed he is dragging me into the bathroom. *Surely it's nicer in this soft bed?*

No, he says, *this is how he wants it this week. It helps him focus.*

That's a new line I haven't heard from anyone before as I concentrate on trying to keep this cruel marble sink from hurting me as he closes his eyes and tells me, *I am a lovely girl, so good and obedient this week. I make him very happy.* He sighs into my hair.

And the same nightmares and him waking up screaming, me having to watch over him and tell him, *the light is on and I am here, he is not alone.* I have to watch over him as he clings to me afraid locked in his night terrors, until finally he is calm and tiredness makes me sleep. I am having nightmares too in the two or three hours that I can sleep, that I am pregnant and he is growing inside me. I wake up in fright. I love him but I am still afraid of what he said to me before, about not wanting me, only a child. I will find I have been tricked and I will go insane, unable to see the child or him. He doesn't realise what savage pain those angry words shouted in our last argument have caused.

The same darkness at 7am, me finding the bed empty and going to see he is okay in the bathroom, I am so worried about his behaviour; him snapping at me to go and then hauling me into the shower, turning me around and having me hard, harder against the cold white tiles under the hot water while my claws scratch the white wall in pain. He is telling me the same thing *that I am a good girl, such a good girl. I am helping him so much.* I feel like this is about the only way I have helped him on this trip as I haven't been much use in the conferences, we haven't networked, he has been too tired. I have just helped him focus by having sex in cold hard places. Some work outing this is. He bites my shoulder and sucks on the wound, licking his lips and looking at me with his eyes full of ecstasy.

I am afraid of what he is and what he has become. I am afraid of what I am becoming. But my heart just will not leave. Not if I travelled to the end of the earth. I would still be his. There is no escape, only infinity and I can choose to accept it or fight it and lose.

We fly back to Oslo in silence. Whatever I try to say he won't answer, he just stares out of the window. He is not really all there and I wish he would see a shrink. I have done nothing wrong this week. I am worried sick about not taking my pill since May. All he has done is shout at me that he wants a child, he is ready now and if I don't want it, I can leave it with him and just go. I feel so disposable as though they would rip the child out of me and hand it to him and he would be out of the operating theatre door while they stitch up my wound. And then I wouldn't see him or the child again. I can't get the image out of my head of jumping into the Duna river after he has cut me out of his life once I have served my purpose.

I am crying against the window, silent tears of the Damned. It breaks his silence.

"Baby, what is it?" He takes my hand and tries to turn me towards him.

I won't turn.

"Hey, what is it? Darling please tell me." He is so soft now. His soul is back in his body.

"I'm afraid you will take the child and leave me and I will never see either of you again. I am so scared about the things you said," I am crying as I tell him. "It hurts so much. And my body hurts so much, you were so rough."

He pulls me into him and tells me *he was angry, he is angry with himself now for saying that, he is angry with himself for hurting me physically, he promises he will never, ever do that again.*

He strokes my hair and says that, *he only said those cruel things to shock me into reality. He wants my reality to be with him and knows he was horrible, he can't say sorry enough. He would never, ever do that, he needs me but he is scared that I would run away and leave him with the child. I am the one who would leave him devastated,* he says. *He can't deal with the emotions I make him feel. No one made him feel the way I do. He knows he says cruel things and he is so sorry afterwards. It hurts him so much.*

I let him hold me tight; I surrender.

What a fucked up King and Queen.

He will show me, he promises, *right now. He will show me what he says is true.*

"Show me what?" I ask as the plane is touching down in Oslo Gardemoen. "Show me what?"

I will take my flight back to Madrid a few hours later and he flies back to Hungary on an earlier flight. And what does he need to show me to make me feel better?

I tell him I will call him, can he give me his phone number which he still hasn't done.

"No," he tells me in Gardemoen airport. "You were not a good girl. You are still going back to all these men in Spain."

I tell him I will come back to Hungary right now if he wants. There is no man or men in Spain.

He tells me, *to go, just like everyone else. Leave, just like they all do in the end.*

"I am not everybody else," I tell him. "I am not

them, I would never be like them, don't you see? I don't care about the bad, I only see the good in you." I am crying as I shout this through the airport and then I am walking away incredibly sad then he runs after me. Show me what? He never showed me.

He chases me and grabs my arm. His eyes are wild. "Come in here, now!" he pulls me into a Swarovski shop. He points at the rings. "I need one of those!" he snaps at the shop assistant who is a pretty blonde Norwegian girl. "Hurry up!" he yells at her as she unlocks the cabinet.

She apologises and I want to say sorry to her for his rude behaviour.

He is running out of time for his flight and he grabs my right hand and finds the biggest diamond in my size and jams it on my wedding finger.

"What are you doing?" I ask him. He doesn't answer but pulls out a load of notes and hands them over and pulls me out of the shop without a word.

"Now will you come back to me? I bought you this. Isn't that what you want? You want to be my wife, don't you? You want to have my children don't you?" He is angry and desperate at the same time and he is going to miss his flight.

"Don't you see, Kiára? Don't you fucking get it?"

Stupid idiot, I think. After this week I might end up with his kid and then what will he do? I am stupid too. We are both fucking careless. I can just imagine us both screaming at each other while the kid screams in the background.

And this is the least romantic engagement I could ever imagine. I just don't know what to say.

"Do you want me? Do you really?" I am trying to stay calm as we leave the shop and he is looking at his watch. "You never wanted anyone before," I tell him.

"You just said you wanted a beautiful child and I could go once that was done. How do I trust you after that?"

"Yes I want you and no I never wanted anyone before and I was angry with you when I said what I did, I am sorry. Go, do whatever you have to do but come back to me. I want you to stop running and stay with me always. I am not giving you my phone number until you do."

"I will come back, I promise," I am running now, but after him to his departure gate.

They are already calling him as the last passenger for his flight.

"István don't just leave like this," I am telling him.

He is still angry and walking fast without looking at me. He gets to his gate and hands over his boarding card. My flight is not for another 2 hours. I think he is just going to go through without even looking at me and on to the plane, then he just drops his bag and lifts me into his arms and presses his face into my hair and whispers, "I love you, I love you so much I could die, my darling."

Before I can say anything he drops me like a discarded toy and he has disappeared through the gate and down the air bridge as if it never happened.

He is the last one on and I hear the stewardess slam the door to the plane.

I am just standing there with this huge diamond on my hand.

Evidence this happened otherwise I would think I dreamed the whole thing. He is half-crazy but I want him so much, more than I ever wanted anything or anyone.

I get back to Tenerife and open my suitcase and put stuff away. I see the useless contraceptive pills in my top drawer and think how stupid I was not to start them up again after the last worry I had. I cover them up and hope that I am as infertile as I think I am. It's Christmas and New Year and I really couldn't care less. It's better here where in the sun you can forget all about it and lie on the beach and eat home-made paella and drink wine on the terrace. I post István some volcanic cufflinks and hope they get to him. Now and then he calls me but from a private number. I ask him, *why doesn't he just give me his phone number, I won't call him a lot, I just would like to send him a text now and then and call him now and then too.* He knows my control, he knows I am not going to be calling him to check up 20 times a day. He knows that about me. However much I want to call, I have self-control in this way.

"Maybe, if you are good girl and come back to me, but not now," he tells me and hangs up.

Damn him to Hell.

I have the diamond on my hand which all the travellers in Tenerife are asking me about and how did he propose to me and I have to say he didn't he just bought me this and ran on to his flight. I still haven't got his goddamn phone number. I have no idea what he is doing or who he is doing but it seems to be all work. He doesn't even know it is Christmas Day when he calls me. I really want to go back to him but I don't want him to feel he has won.

Where are his relatives? Where is he from? Why is he alone on Christmas Day? I know nothing apart from the birthplace on his passport listed as Debrecen, Hungary.

Nothing gets to me on this rock. My mother's chocolate she posts to me gets lost, or more like eaten by the Correos. I lean over the balcony and talk to the beautiful silky black rooster next door who struts along with his red comb on his head, a king surrounded by his harem of hens. He puts his head on one side to listen to me and I wonder if I am losing my mind. I seem to have a permanent glass of wine in my hand these days. I go to bed with some sleeping pills on New Year's Eve and everyone else makes the 8km trip into Puerto de la Cruz where they are ripped off, drunk and then stranded until the next morning. New Year's Day is the one day of the year where I can usually guarantee a hangover free day as I never go out.

A Finnish girl staying in the house doesn't go out either. She arrives early evening on New Year's eve crying. I always have an affinity with the Finns and their language sounds like ice crystals forming. Although their tongue is part of the Finno-Ugric family, she can't understand my Hungarian and I can't understand a word of Finnish. She tells me she has been staying higher up the mountainside at someone's miserable farm with neglected animals and sorry-looking horses. The walk down here took 2 hours and she is depressed. She came over here to feel better and to escape the vicious cold winter. I tell her about my Norwegian excursion, show her the diamond and she stops crying and starts laughing and laughing.

"That is so fucked up," she says.

I know, I know. I show her the picture frame of István and she studies it carefully.

"But what the hell, he is so handsome. A little mad maybe but what a gorgeous guy. Don't let him go," she tells me.

"I won't," I say. I look at the photo again. He is so beautiful I can't expect normality. I don't want to let him go, ever.

A few days' later my time of the month is late again and I feel sad. I look at his photo and suddenly realise I do want his kid and never had this feeling for someone before. I have a vision of a beautiful little version of him with black silk curls and dark lovely eyes and a trusting smile, a gorgeous little boy. We get out the toy dinosaurs and play......

You stupid cow, Kiára. Then I slam the drawer and think, *to hell with that, what a crazy idea, you crazy bitch.* I crack open another bottle of wine on the terrace. *He is nuts, I am bipolar, God help the kid.* We are not fit between us to take care of a houseplant. We would do something like forget the kid was there, leave it outside a restaurant and go home or leave it in the car in the heat of summer until it dies like a neglected dog.

Me and the Finnish girl get so drunk and dance on the roof terrace one night until she falls into the giant cactus in the corner. Despite the pain she must be in we are killing ourselves laughing. The Scandinavians love these Spanish islands with the insanely cheap alcohol. The other residents come back and find us both still drinking wine and beer laughing like crazy, me with a pair of tweezers in my hand pulling out the giant cactus spikes from her ass and thighs while my computer plays out dance tunes.

I know once I hit beer bottles I am beyond drunk. I hate beer. We all crack open more beer and turn the music up.

Damn you, István, I don't need you.

I will have a hangover tomorrow, but somehow they are less savage here, just a dull fuzz, nothing a few churros and strong coffee can't sort out until the next night.

I remember the visions I kept having in Lanzarote the year before when I was with the violent man from Valencia. I drove around the uninhabited areas of the island towards El Golfo where the jet black landscape is like the surface of the moon and there's an emerald green lake. I kept paying to go into the Cesar Manrique foundation where he built his house in five lava bubbles as I loved the deceased artist's work. But the diesel car I hired stalled in the centre of the windchime roundabout and I saw visions of him in my head as cars headed towards me. Everything went slow and silent and I wondered if this was the end. I later found out this was the same roundabout he had died at in a road traffic accident. The Valencian made me drive as he wanted to sample the wines in the vineyards, so I drove through jet black land under a bright blue sky which cuts through the centre of the island. White bodegas pepper the route and I had to watch him drink the finest volcanic wines on offer while I sat there with nothing. *What am I, your fucking taxi-driver?*

But I also had visions of someone like István through all my dreams, someone I never knew, someone I needed. I started pushing the twin beds further and further apart as though I couldn't bear the man I was with to touch me. I dreamed of István long before I met him and even before I left the violent Valencian I didn't want him near me at night. I wanted my head to be clear for this handsome stranger who was in my dreams long before he was in my life.

SÖTÉT VÁROS

My body is always tricked by the two months I spend in the Canary Islands each winter. I wake up one morning in Tenerife in mid January in fright and in pain and there are trails of blood all over the bed. I was so drunk last night, I don't remember if I fell in a giant cactus and that's when I realise I have had another miscarriage. I am fucked up beyond belief as I cry in the blood-stained bed, the remains of our savage love all over my legs and sheets, cramp crushing my middle and I start taking my contraceptive pill immediately, I cannot go through this again. I don't go to the medical centre although I should as I am bleeding for days. I just swallow a load of codeine and hit the bottle of wine once it is a reasonable time in the late afternoon as I am due to fly back the next day.

When I arrive back in Hungary in winter, it's always brutal. Instead of the golden light and parched land and white buildings and bright flowers, the ride from the airport is nothing but grey. Slushy snow is piled up in shades of blackish grey at the roadside. For some idiot reason I can't explain I decide I will stay in Budapest and travel down to Pécs to see István and I find a dark apartment for cut price in a grim bit of the VIII district. This was not the plan. I arrived in Pécs to see him all happy, ready to stay with him and try to stop the craziness and the arguments, only to be told *just because I am engaged to him, doesn't mean we have to live together yet*. He says this in a cruel way. This made me so mad I got the first train back to Budapest, which in turn made him even madder as he didn't expect me to do that. I am sickly due to blood loss, anaemic and I can see by my inner eyelids that despite my tan I am deathly pale.

I pass out twice the second day in work and earlier that day, on the metro in Budapest. István is worried and takes me to the doctor in Pécs who rightly diagnoses me with anaemia. I keep quiet as to the cause. I am stupid, I could have haemorrhaged and died. The doctor says I have to take a course of iron and I need blood right now, I am dangerously anaemic. István says he will give me his and as this is his friend, Zsolt, I am given the blood there and then.

Are you both crazy? I shout. *You can't just.....*

The needle is already in my fat vein. I am too weak to care.

I lie to Zsolt and say I just don't eat enough, can't tell him the truth. It is strange we are both O negative, a rare group here. As I watch the dark fluid drip into my body, I feel a strange sort of feeling maybe due to being ill. It is as though he has found another way to possess me, entering me through my veins, filling my body with his blood, this vampire. I know that Zsolt is trying to help without hospitalising me and our blood has been screened before so there are no risks. All the same it is not normal medical practice and I wonder if everyone around me is going insane. I try to shake the surreal image out of my head as István is only helping me, he is right to be worried and offer his blood. I look at the dark eyes of the man who is giving me his life fluid and they are depthless. He has no expression. I have to look away from the intensity and then he scoops me up and I am carried back to his car gently and he makes me rest in his apartment.

As I am drifting away I feel his weight on the bed.

"What the Hell did you do this time, baby, what did you do to yourself?" István says. He examines my body for wounds as I am sleeping but finds none. He is convinced I self-harmed badly and bled a lot in Spain but he is mystified when he finds no evidence. I want to tell him the truth but I can't right now.

When I feel a bit better I head back to the dark city and my dark apartment. The apartment is cut price because there are no windows in the living room or bathroom. Only the bedroom has a window onto the courtyard but the bars on the front give me nightmares about being in prison. Plus all the space in the apartment is in the height. When a lightbulb pops, I can't reach it on a stepladder, so I end up buying a lot of candles. In this apartment, I don't know if it's day or night, summer or winter. In my head it is always winter these days. I am getting awful sleep paralysis. I wake up and look around the room and can't speak or move my limbs. It seems to last a lifetime but it could only be a minute. If I don't get up, I will slide back into my nightmares, of which there are many. This must be what locked-in syndrome is like. Despite all the energy I summon to try to move my arms and legs, I can't and I am awake and paralysed. A doctor tells me it is one of my antidepressants doing this, a side effect.

My bipolar is raging out of control. I'm afraid of jumping under the 4/6 tram so I try to take buses instead. I do not want to die pancaked on the tracks. Especially not at Blaha Lujza Tér.

István is asking me why I'm in Budapest, why I'm not in Pécs. Who is in Budapest? Where am I staying? He doesn't trust me. The truth is I am too afraid of his hard heart and being hurt again. He has already shouted he only took me out for dates out of pity, he only gave me work out of pity and I am engaged to him only because I wanted it and this has made me so angry I am keeping my distance. I know it's not true as he is so defensive but part of me doesn't. I don't know what to believe anymore. I know I am engaged to him because he wants it, after all I never asked. He is the one who dragged me into the shop in Gardemoen airport and bought me an engagement ring.

Only now he is behaving like an asshole. If my heart wasn't already trapped and if he wasn't so beautiful, I would tell him to stick his ring where the sun doesn't shine, or better go and sell it. More than once I actually remove it and hand it back to him when he has been so impossible. But he simply takes my hand and puts it back on.

"No," he says. "This is yours and when you are ready you will come to me. You need to learn love, sweetheart. It is not in your wild nature."

Insulting bastard. He who spent most of his life alone waiting for his goddamn Queen of Hungary.

I spend all my money I would have saved as I am never in my dark apartment. I sit in coffee houses across the city writing on my computer or in my friend's bar drinking the evening and my misery away. I also hate the VIII district, why in Hell's name am I here? I should be in the districts I like; the XII, the I and the II all on the Buda side. The VIII is full of hobos by the metro station and although it's safe enough I am sick of the old homeless witch with no teeth who keeps calling me a whore and spitting bread at the people on the street. So I spend more time in my friend's bar.

I am falling apart fast. I am on the train to northern Hungary one day when our train slows down to a crawl. We are in one of those old international trains heading to Berlin and it has six-seater compartments and a corridor running alongside. It is early morning and a Hungarian man opposite me is reading a book whilst me and a Slovakian man are gazing at the view when we see a heap of something on the railtrack next to our train. Before I can look away, I see a mass of chopped up limbs and a torso and a head, man or woman, blood and bone and hair.

The Slovak says something in his language like "Oh my God," and runs to throw up. I fight the nausea rising in my gut. I just think about the desperation of the poor person who was so depressed they lay across the tracks waiting for the early morning Prague to Budapest to slice them into pieces. I know how they must have felt and this makes it worse. The violence of the method shocks me as I consider jumping into rivers or taking pills suicide, not this gruesome end. Gruesome ends are not in my lexicon.

The Slovak returns and says, *he has to go to the bar car and take some pills or something, he can't get the image out of his head.*

I know I will never get the image out of mine. And I never do. I can never eat meat again after this. I cannot even eat red food as it is the colour of blood. I reluctantly prepare István meat dishes as he has a theory that us blood group O negatives need more meat than other types as we are closer to ancient men. *Well he is anyway; he is still a caveman.*

On the Budapest to Pécs train the next day I see a small marble crucifix and fresh flowers by the railtrack. Another case, another train track suicide. It makes me cry. At times like this I question what I am doing in a country where suicide is so common. *Why aren't I back in Spain where the people are lighter, happier?*

And yet, it makes me crazy. Here in Hungary, people understand sadness. I can travel away and yet I am always propelled back here after a month or so, like some crazy boomerang.

One night there is a fancy dress party. I am drinking more to forget everything this dark winter. I have some wine, a couple of pastries and 4 or 5 shots of pálinka over the whole evening and one minute I am dancing with Santa and a martian covered in blue balloons, the next I hit the floor. My friend laughs and carries me upstairs where I throw up violently until there's nothing left of me. I can't move for 2 days and question him about his source of pálinka from my flat position in his bed. I'm poisoned and he spends the night picking up cowboys, fairies and other characters from the bar floor and the garden. He gets mad and tells me *his pálinka is always good, it's not surprising I am poisoned given all the pills I take and I never eat and anyway this is just a normal Hungarian party, everyone sick on pálinka.*

This is not normal. This is not good.

That winter I get involved with men all over Budapest, I get into their cars because they seem nice and because I meet them in coffee bars. I am hurting István indirectly but really I am only hurting myself. I am too proud to go back to live in Pécs. I don't care about my safety. I forget their names or I don't even ask, I go out with their friends, my friends and back in a circle to the first man I started with. The only thing I know is that I am not having sex. I am always too drunk, they are always too drunk and I fall asleep in my clothes wrapping the sheet around me like a shroud. It's not bringing me happiness and I am doing it to forget István but it's not working. I am still sleeping next to his picture with Lana Del Rey playing in a loop until I fall asleep. Our meetings in Pécs are full of strife. I am wasting hours every week getting the train from Budapest to go to work and sometimes he lets me stay in his apartment, sometimes not.

This up and down, the moods we are both in is driving us both crazy. I just want to stay with him and not have to put on this act.

He wants to know why I am in Budapest, what I am doing and more importantly who am I doing. He is raging with jealousy and yet he won't commit. I tell him does he want his diamond back as he is behaving like he does but he says no, I can keep it and when I am good and well-behaved I will be his wife and mother of his children. Right now I am not a good example and I scream at him take a look in the mirror and see why you don't have any kids.

"You may be beautiful, István, but God, you are fucked up! No woman would stay with you longer than one nightmare filled night."

He turns to me burning with anger and hurt. "Bitch," he says. This has touched a raw nerve.

I am in his apartment at the time and he locks himself in the bathroom after this and won't come out for 3 hours. I can hear him crying inside and it is breaking my heart. I plead with him to open the door. I am so sorry.

"I am so sorry, I am a bitch, please come out. I don't care about the nightmares, I want to take care of you. Now and forever. Let me take care of you, please," I call through the keyhole.

I sit there and listen to him and he won't speak, won't even shout at me, which at least would be something. I am telling him, *I am here and I want to hold him.*

I have to go to bed in the end. He won't come out. I wake up and he is there, a shadowy figure in the half-light with his black curls wild and uncombed, his face streaked with tears. What is wrong with him? I thought he was the heartbreaker when I first met him, in control, unaffected by emotions.

"You hurt me, you don't want me, I am just nothing to you. I never wanted anyone to be close to me before and here I am wanting a kid with you so desperately. What you said hurt me so much," he says.

In the half dark I pull him into the bed. "Nothing, I am nothing to you," he is saying. "You are a cruel woman with no heart. I thought when I first saw you that you were lovely and sweet and would be a kind loving mother. Nothing is further from the truth. Your beauty is hard and cold like your diamond."

"No, it isn't true. Darling, István, you are everything to me, everything," I tell him.

"I want you too and I need you here with me, I am afraid," he is saying.

"I am here, I am here. You don't need to be afraid, I will be here through all the dark nights." Even as I say it, even as he squeezes hold of me and starts running his hands along my back, as he is so afraid of the darkness in his head and my body is Heaven to him, I know the next morning he won't be afraid. He won't need me.

Maybe we should both be committed to an asylum. This is so fucked up beyond belief. We argue a lot, screaming and shouting but unlike any other man I never feel it is the end. We will never be at the end. I feel like we are in each others' blood. Sometimes I catch him looking at me when I am working in the dental surgery; standing in the doorway with such sadness in his eyes, unable to take his eyes off me and his mouth ready to say what I want him to say.

Or not. He always turns away when I look up and leaves the room. This is the most fucked up engagement I could ever have dreamt up. I wouldn't even imagine it could be so bad.

At the end of February, I stop picking up men in Budapest as it is doing me no good. I can't bear to be with anyone unless it's István. And I feel awful as I know he is not cheating on me, never would and it would break his heart if he knew what I was doing, although I kid myself I am not cheating if I am just dating and passing out in their beds. I am breaking my own heart doing what I am doing and it is horrible, but whenever he hurts me I come back to Budapest and cheat.

He comes up to Budapest and surprises me one weekend; he has come to get me and take me out of this dark world and dark apartment. He is packing my suitcase for me to take me home. I also think he was hoping to catch me being unfaithful. I am half-guilty as I have been kind of cheating and I am engaged to him and yet half-angry that he is still been pushing me away from him since I returned from Spain. He sees my gloomy apartment and says "Baby, what are you doing here, in this God-forsaken place. You shouldn't be alone like this. You should be with me."

But the next morning he is cold again and uncaring. I ask him, *why he is so nasty today?*

I am making coffee with my café mocha machine on the stovetop. He is sullen all day and eventually he snaps and reveals the cause of his anger and he holds up my contraceptive pill packet he has found in the bathroom cabinet. He says, *I am taking this so I can fuck around. This is sickening, don't I know how much he paid for that diamond?*

I tell him, *I am taking it to be responsible, something he doesn't bother about and didn't care about in but left me worrying about the consequences while he is lost in his teeth and work as usual.*

I stopped taking the pill in May and each month I am worried so I started taking it again to stop the worry, something he doesn't have to even think about.

He says, *he is responsible and he is responsible enough to be a parent and he is ready for a kid now. He wasn't ready before but he feels ready now. It is the right time for him.*

He is so arrogant.

Like hell, I tell him.

Unlike you, he says to me in disgust. *You are not fit to be a mother. I know why you are here in Budapest, just for sex. Your daughter would be a whore like you.*

"Don't forget she would be messed up having you for a father. She would only turn tricks to get away from you because you are so horrible! And you are such a twisted bastard you would probably try and fuck her yourself!"

He looks like he has been burned. He steps back. This is nasty. I don't mean it but he thinks I do and he grabs my arm and tells me, *I am fucking sick to think that, to say that to him.*

I also add, *and yeah and there are plenty of men for me in this city.*

This is also a stupid thing to say.

Yes but I only want you, I think.

He holds my diamond up to the light or rather the electric light as there is no natural light in this dark living space, and says, "You ungrateful bitch." His eyes are full of rage. He opens my suitcase and tips all the clothes out and then pulls all my contraceptive pills out of the cabinet and throws them in the garbage, then to make sure he bags it up and takes it with him.

"I'm sorry, I didn't mean that. I only want you," I am pleading now. I am so stupid living here, doing what I am doing.

"Liar," he is walking out of the door. "Stay here for all I care in your dark apartment with your dark heart, lady. How dare you say I would want sex with my own daughter? You are one fucked up bitch."

"István, I'm sorry," I am chasing him down the marble stairs into the courtyard. "Let me come with you, please."

He doesn't speak, he is crying angry hard tears and he just pushes me away, gets in his car in the street and drives away. I run after its angry fast blackness in the street in my bare feet and thin dress.

He is gone.

I am standing there in the cold in the miserable VIII district. A cold hard diamond. A homeless man asks me for 20 forints. "Nem," I say, "nem."

I look like a crazy person myself with just a silk nightdress on and no shoes in the cold.

I messed this one up this time. I could have been out of here and with him if I hadn't started the goddamn pill again or at least hidden it someplace. And to say those hurtful things which in no way I believed, just to cut him open and hurt him. To hurt the man I love more than life itself.

Hell, could my life get any more messed up.

The answer is yes. It reminds me of a university lecturer who was talking about philosophers defining the absolute, but what if there is no absolute. You think you have hit rock bottom and then the cliff falls on your head, there is never an end. It was about infinity.

Which is exactly the word I always think of when I think of István.

Infinity.

I cry myself to sleep that night and pop a load of benzos. I feel I have ruined everything.

*I get a text which wakes me up an hour later. He must have stopped halfway back to the south. **I am sorry. You would be a lovely mother. I am a jealous man. I love you.***

I want to text him back to say I am sorry, I never meant to say what I did and I cannot be a lovely mother when I keep punishing my body and having miscarriages and he doesn't even know about this latest one, but I can't put it into words. I can't do anything. He then calls me from the private number; he is sitting in his car halfway home so upset by the things he said and he doesn't know whether he can drive home without me.

I tell him through my tears, *I had another miscarriage in January and I started the pill again because I am so messed up. It has given me anaemia, which is why I am so weak.* I am crying so much and he is silent. I am a wreck and I keep trying to hold my vulnerability from him. I am crying like my world is ending in this prison of an apartment.

"I am coming back to get you. I am coming now," he says.

I am still in my dress with bare feet and he scoops back the clothes into my case and carries me and the suitcase out into the street. We don't say a word but he strokes my face and his eyes say everything he needs to say, everything I need to say. It is 3am something and I don't know why we are both acting so crazy, only love makes you crazy. We drive wordlessly back south into blackness and he just holds my hand as we drive. We are beyond speaking.

He makes me stay in bed the next day while he calls his doctor friend again after he is shocked I didn't see a doctor in Spain and refused to tell the truth when he took me to the doctor in Pécs after I collapsed in work. *I could have died*, he tells me. He turns away to hide his emotions.

I lie there broken and useless in his kingsize bed. He tells me later, *the doctor has said it is stress, alcohol, low body weight and generally not taking care of myself.*

I have to start being healthy.

He says to me, *he is so upset I have had now had two miscarriages and I am alone and only tell him later. Don't know it is his loss too and we should be comforting each other? Don't I realise this time I could have died as I never went to the medical centre or the hospital when it happened unlike last time in Spain.*

It is his birthday two days later and I conveniently forget it, 28 February. I am in the dental surgery working that day and I tell him, *I couldn't sleep for the cruel words I said in Budapest two nights' ago, I said them to hurt him and I never meant to do it.* He just nods and accepts my apology and yet I decline to go for drinks with him and the rest of the staff saying I have other arrangements. I don't even give him a gift although I had bought one as I was hoping today we would be okay with each other. He is so visibly hurt. I walk out of the door and go to his apartment. He watches me walk away and I feel a sense of happiness to hurt him. I shouldn't feel this.

This is not love, it is sickness.

The reason I am so angry is because he has happily told everyone I am his fiancée and they wonder what we are doing being so nasty to each other and why I am not living with him officially. He tells them, *we have plenty of time to live together, I am a wild horse and I haven't been tamed yet.*

Then he laughs and says, *he is going to tame me given time.*

I assumed I was living there now. I have already told him how sorry I am for my nasty comments about molesting his own daughter but I know he is angry and still wants to hurt me back. He says this comment about taming me in work to the other staff and it is this nasty remark which makes me walk out the door and throw the gift I got for him in the bin in the street and fuck his birthday.

In fact, fuck Hungary. I am so mad.

He comes back from the bar and finds me in bed having cried myself to sleep, he rolls my sleeve back and he sees burns. Fresh burns I did to myself to ease the pain and he says this has to stop, he will not let me do this. He is angry, really angry but he kisses the burns and rubs his face against me telling me, *I have to stop for him.*

"Don't you know how much this hurts me, baby?" he says. "Don't you have any idea how much pain I feel that do this to yourself?"

I tell him, *I am sorry, I will stop, I promise.*

It's a particularly brutal winter. Spring has always arrived early in the time I have been in Hungary and March can be warm but this year, the winter whips up a blizzard on March 15 and I decide to return to Latvia after a half-promise of some work. I tell István and he twists his hands into a knot as he is treating my jaw at the time. I say it so casually, that I am just going for a month or so.

He looks at me and says. "What is wrong with you?

I can't do nothing for you and your jaw when you are away. And you should be here with me, I bought you that diamond so you would stay, what can I do to make you stay? If you stopped all this running away you would not have had two miscarriages, you would not be so thin, you say I push you away but you do it even worse to me."

"You could stop playing games and just let me stay for good in your apartment for a start. Why can't you do that?" I ask him. "You want to tame me? Go ahead, but you have to let me in to do that and I can't see that ever happening!"

He pulls at his latex gloves, stretching them out of shape. He blows one into a cow's udder and sits there holding it. "You can stay," he says quietly. I stare into those endless eyes of his that change from darkest brown to black like a human mood ring. He won't say anything else. I get up. He is still sitting there.

I hug him and whisper into his black curls, *I will be back, it is only one month, maximum two and I will come back I promise* and he squeezes me tighter and then we let go and I get up.

I am leaving my heart behind. I must be going insane.

What the Hell am I trying to prove? He already told me if I don't work much, he can take care of me and in the Spring there will be tourists arriving for dental work and I will be busy again.

And this is for you, I tell him. I leave it on the counter. It is the gift I bought him for his birthday and retrieved from the bin as it seemed stupid to waste money like that.

I hear him tearing it open so fast as he does with gifts.

"*Kiára......*" he calls after me. I know this gift was

very special to him. But I am gone. I go straight to the airport, there is no chance he can follow me as he has a full day until 8pm.

I love him more than I ever thought possible. I love him for his everything; his faults, his fuckups and the light and beauty which shine through all this. He is like Sicily; the sun shines brighter, yet the shadows are darker. I don't care what he did wrong, what he will do wrong in years to come. I will love him until the day I die. My István; my one and only. My darling. If he is not there, there will be no one to compare to István, the first king of Hungary.

Latvia can't be any worse than this and I haven't had much work since Christmas. I just want to show István that I can do a month or two without him and then I plan to go back, just to prove a point. Oh, but it is worse. I'd forgotten the biting wind razoring in through the streets straight from the Baltic, the winter that lingers until June. It has become worse in the time I have been away as the rich Russians have moved in from Moscow, buying property in Jurmala and pushing up rental prices in Riga. I go to look at an overpriced guesthouse which is as expensive as Western Europe. It's in Purciems. I don't know this district and the further the bus goes into the uniform grey of Soviet housing blocks, I don't really want to. After half an hour in deepest Purciems the bus driver says to me "It's the end of the line, lady."

I can see that. It looks more like the end of the world.

I am crying. I answer in Russian. "I'm lost."

"Stay on the bus," she says kindly. "I'll have a cigarette and in 10 minutes, I'll drive back to the city."

This isn't what it was like when I was here all those years ago. I lived in old Riga, near the Powder

Tower as I can't bear to live in grim districts. I would sooner spend virtually all my money on my rent than live in a sketchy area. I never even ventured into those suburbs although I saw names like Dole and Zolitude as I passed them on the train. Rows and rows of identical grey housing blocks with only a tobacco shop in the middle. The lonely name describes it all; Zolitude.

This brings me to where I am lying on my back in the snow in Lithuania, half-crazy, drifting like the flakes that are falling all around me, running from country to country to avoid my feelings; country hopping, man swapping, bar flopping, pill popping. What happened to me? I am flying from hot to cold and back again. As I watch planes cross diagonally below me in the sky from my window seat, I imagine my alter-ego sitting in them gazing back at me. I am spending so much on airfare I should have shares in Ryanair. I have become an expert in carrying as much baggage as I can and hiding everything under my fur coat.

"Save me István!" I scream from the snowy street. The sound is muffled by the thick white all around me. "Please save me. I love you! I forgive you everything!"

Some travellers from the hostel see me as I lie in the snow near the entrance.

"She is crazy," one of them says to the others.

"The world is crazy," I shout from my position in the snow. "Not me!"

Lithuania is worse than Latvia, I was hoping it would be better. I have come here for no reason other than I am melting down. On the coach from the border all the way to Vilnius I don't see a single house, animal or person only endless fields and trees of white. It is literally as though the last person in the country left and turned out the lights. I cry on the coach not caring about the people around me. Yes, they look at me but with that understanding you only find in Eastern Europe. It is okay to be sad. It is okay to cry and you can get on with it.

Once I was crying so much on a bus in Budapest, an older lady touched my arm and asked "Segíthetek? Hogy vagy?"

I thanked her and said, *no it is okay. I don't need help but I am just sad today and thanks for asking.*

She nodded, understanding. Yes, it is okay to be sad and to cry in public is not a weakness.

In the UK people would look at me like I am crazy.

I am so depressed I forget the clocks go forward and miss my flight out of Vilnius, so I will have to go back to Riga to get another cheap one. As I am staying in bed for the three nights I am in Lithuania, the other travellers in the hostel are curious. They find me a bit mad but entertaining.

They ask "Won't you join us, Kiára, we are sitting drinking in the kitchen?"

The kitchen is too cold but one Japanese boy lifts me up from the bed as I am so light and carries me and my duvet down to the kitchen where he sets me down and gives me a big glass of wine.

I see a girl I met in Riga years ago and she is pleased to see me. She is studying in Sweden and gets out her bottle of wine. This gets me through the nights I am there; my duvet and a load of wine. Until 4.30am that is which is when I wake up and everyone in my dorm room is asleep and I am frenzied and the snow is thick outside the window and making everything silent.

4.30am is one of the worst times to wake up in the

world. I have some idea that maybe 3am is worse, or 3.45am but then it depends totally where you are and who you are with and can you get up and watch TV or take a load of klonopin and a milkshake, or best curl up to István and his warm body. Oh, I need him so much in the night as I know this is also the time he needs me with his night terrors and his fear of the dark he won't discuss. I am confused as the hour went forward on the flight and then again the other night. So it is really 2.30am. I think.

I think in my head and hope it reaches him *My darling, I miss you more than I could ever say. I want to be with you.*

He is probably asleep so my phone surprises me 5 minutes later when I get a text from a Hungarian number. Well I hope it is him as it is not a number I recognise. He still wants to keep his phone private until now, which has driven me insane.

I can't lie in this bed without you. Without you I am nothing. Please come back and never leave.

The sentiments are there but he knows I can't call him at this time of night. I also have virtually no credit on my phone. I should be happy my thoughts reached him, I should call him but I can't.

I just text back *I want to be there so much. I want to be with you now.*

I feel so helpless as the snow shrouds the outside world in a blanket of silence and everyone is asleep apart from me and I feel so far from my István.

I return to Latvia and decide to make myself as depressed as possible to appreciate Hungary more. I know now that I can't stay in Latvia and work, not even for a month. It is making me sicker and I have to go back home. I visit Daugavpils which is near the Russian border and boasts more prisons than churches. On a tram in this god-forsaken place I pass a prison that is straight out of the Gulag. Stark white in the snow, razor wire, watchtowers, an exercise track running between walls, windows with bars and no glass. I visit the Rothko museum where the staff kindly take me around and stand to wave me goodbye as I leave in the swirling snowstorm. I remember Rothko committed suicide by slashing his wrists. In New York, I think.

I go back to the hotel I am spending the night in and peer out of the window. They won't let me use the sauna and spa as it is booked by an Estonian wedding party. Fucking weddings. There is no point arguing with the Russians on the desk even though I am only the third guest in their hotel. Why would anyone be in frozen wasteland in the snow for any kind of pleasure?

Next door a scratchy looking dog and a broken house with a corrugated iron roof make me feel as depressed as I can get. I close the curtains and go and sit in the bar and drink a bottle of cheap Russian champagne to forget the darkness and cold. The next morning I throw my guts up in the bathroom. I have a feeling of heaviness inside that I put down to the smoked salmon pancakes.

Passing through the frozen wilderness from Daugavpils back to Riga I see broken huts and more half-starved dogs. On one station wall in the ass-end of nowhere someone has daubed in red paint **Drugs set you free.** I can't argue with that. Two miserable mongrels watch our slow train pass by.

A text comes through; **Please come home to me. Szeretlek.** It is from him. I cry out of happiness this time.

I text him back. **I will be there on Tuesday. No more running. Please call me, I am really sick.**

Szeretlek. Mindig.

He calls me immediately and I tell him, *I am dying without him. I am really sick with this bipolar and my chest infection.* It is the first time I mention bipolar to him but then he would have known that, he would have figured it out for himself.

He just tells me, *get some antibiotics, get the first plane, no matter the cost, he will pay. He needs me and he needs me in Pécs in his apartment with him. No more games, no more jealousy, no more pushing me away, he gives me his word.*

"I am not easy, I am not easy to live with but we can work it out. I promise you I will never ask you to leave my apartment again. If I lose you I die," he tells me. "I missed you so much at night when I have my bad dreams and there is no Kiára to hold me and to tell me it is okay. I missed you so much, darling. I don't care how difficult it is or if you scream at me every night, I need you. I love you."

I have a chest infection so when I am waiting for my plane in Riga airport I am sweating like a drug mule despite the cold and nearly hallucinating. I am surprised they don't stop me getting on the plane. I go via Stockholm Skavsta and I collapse in the airport hotel room bed trying to sleep off the sickness. István calls me and I say, *I am not a good girl. I am crying, I am sick and I am coming back tomorrow.*

I am rambling and I say, *I love him and I will never leave Hungary again.*

REMÉNY

Skorpió

**You are trapped in
Amber**

**Suspending your prayer
In a pyramid
Forever about to strike**

István picks me up from the train station. I haven't
let go of my amber pyramid with its scorpion that I
picked up from Latvia for the whole journey. I am
only carrying one small suitcase. I keep leaving my
clothes scattered across Europe. In Hungary, in
Spain, in Latvia. Half the time I can't remember
where they are, what I've lost, where I left them and
why. Half the time they don't fit in the case so I
donate clothes to people I meet en route. If I don't get
some stability in my life now I am really going to lose
my mind and not just my clothes.

"It's good to see you," I say to him

"It's good to see you too," he says shyly. He's
wearing the amber cuff-links I posted from Latvia.

We sit there for a minute and then I collapse into
his arms.

I cry and cry and I can't stop and I say, "I need you.
I need you so much. I always needed you."

He says "It's okay. It's okay to need someone."

I just keep repeating into his chest, "I'm sorry, I'm
sorry for everything. I made such a mess of
everything. I am an ungrateful bitch, you were right."

"You don't need to be sorry for nothing, we are all

fucked up," he says. "If you're sad, cry."

In one of his moments of tenderness he carries me and my suitcase into his apartment. The chocolate labrador woman is peeping through her curtains at us as I am howling so much. I won't let go of him as I am afraid he will escape and he has to prise my hands off me to go in the kitchen to get us something to eat. I can't let go, I am drowning in his beauty, in his soft creamy skin and black curls and his beautiful eyes with those long black lashes. He has become my God shining in the darkness of my world. I am running a fever and I can't let God out of my sight, I mustn't lose God. I follow him to the kitchen wrapped in a sheet and I follow him to the bathroom, I don't care that I am behaving like a fruitcake, I have no dignity or self-preservation left. If he is angry, let him be. But he isn't. He asks me, *wouldn't I rather just stay in bed than sit on the kitchen floor while he makes something to eat, or at least sit on a chair?*

No, I say. *I am afraid I won't find you again.*

Everything hurts and he gets me some antibiotics despite his dislike of pills as the chest infection is making me cough and cough.

I never get sick, usually once every two years but when I do, I always get a chest infection. Every morning I throw up.

He prises something out of my hands as I have been clutching it all the way back from Latvia. It is my scorpion trapped in a pyramid of amber, fresh from the petrified tree resin of Latvia. "I saw this and I thought of you," I say as he looks at it puzzled.

"So pretty and you have a sting in your tail, and now you are caught in an amber prism."

Then I start to laugh and then I am crying and crying and I can't stop. I feel so bad that he sees me like this.

I cry for 5 hours and he puts me to bed and turns the amber scorpion over and over in his hands and holds it up to the light and says "What are we going to do with you, baby?"

"What are we going to do, baby?" he asks me again.

I don't know. I love you. I think I am talking in my sleep. It must be the fever. *Szeretlek; I love you.*

"What did you say?" he asks me snapping on the light.

"Semmi, semmi," I reply. *Nothing, nothing. Kedvesem.*

Each night I have nightmares and sleep paralysis or I'm talking in my sleep. *Szeretlek, kedvesem. Szeretlek. Mindig.*

He wraps me up in his arms.

"You are way too thin. You're dying, baby." He tells me. There is moisture on my back and I don't know if it is sweat or his tears. It makes him so sad to see me this way, to see me so thin and fragile and depressed, he tells me. I feel his breath on my neck and it feels so good. So good to be encased in him. I never want it to end. I have made up my mind I will not argue this time, I will not ruin everything. He kisses the diamond on my hand. "Promise me you'll stay," he says.

"Always," I murmur.

I haven't eaten much this year and it's April. He has a point that I am way too thin. Some days just a biscuit and a few pieces of sushi.

I don't get out of bed for a week apart from to see him when I hear his key in the door at around 8pm each evening. I leap into his arms still wrapped in a sheet and won't let go. His apartment has turned into an asylum. I wonder if I will really lose the plot and start playing with dolls and barking at the moon.

It's the first time I have let my real vulnerability show and I expected him to be impatient. But he brings me soup when he returns from work. He stuffs everything with as many calories as he can, tipping cream into every dish he brings home. He sits there and just holds me, sometimes spooning the food into my mouth to make sure I eat it. Sitting there afterwards to make sure I don't throw it up. He knows this was an old party trick of mine and it is so unhealthy. I have a vision of his heart opening up and swallowing me and I drown in his blood. He is blood group O negative like me. There are only 0.15% of O negatives like us in Hungary and we can only receive blood from our group, despite being universal donors. We'd need each other in a car crash. I already have his blood circulating through my body after I was so badly anaemic a few months' ago.

I am too tired, too broken to hide all my pills so he sees me popping them as I sit up in bed.

He looks at the pill bottles thoughtfully and says to me, "Spring will be here soon Baby, and summer. You'll feel better, you'll see." He strokes my hair. I want to bottle his tenderness and keep it like a favourite perfume so I can remember it when he lashes out again. I want this István to stay and hold me through my dark dreams as he is doing right now.

I hope I will feel better. Right now I am sick. He knows I am sick. I can't run anymore. I keep hiding my morning sickness from him as he would only think this is something it isn't. I just think I am sick.

The first rays of warmth are in the April air and I get up and go to the Cukrászda for coffee with the trees that are blossoming shaking gently outside. The ice-cream shops are opening their doors. I hate ice-cream but the awful sickness that seemed to have penetrated even my bone marrow seems to be fading, but like nausea I am wary. I know it will return. I am just grateful for any day or hour or minute when I don't feel terrible. The sun feels so good and the warm coloured buildings of Pécs seem so pretty and soft after the harshness of north-eastern Europe and the dark heart of Budapest in winter. I don't want to run anymore. I make up my mind if I am bored out of my skull in this place it is nothing compared to the loneliness, the madness of running around Europe like I've been doing. And my suitcase is in István's wardrobe, the clothes are hanging on his rail. It has been two weeks. I didn't even ask to stay.

He leaves early for work and every morning I crawl to the bathroom and throw my guts up; one May morning, more than usual. I am so sick for so long I am scared I am dying and I never tell him I am afraid I have something seriously wrong with me as I always feel a bit better when he returns in the evening.

I'm so busy religiously pill-popping and avoiding alcohol to try to maintain my spirit level on its delicate balance. I haven't taken my contraceptive pills since István threw them all away when he came to my dark apartment in Budapest and maybe he did me a favour. I was tired of the headaches and I know I'm also way too thin to be fertile, my BMI is underweight. My periods are hardly noticeable but I realise I've not had one since February or was it March, I don't know. I put it down to stress. But I shouldn't still be stressed; I am in István's apartment and I am writing articles. I am working a bit and this moody man has calmed down and become soft and gentle. I'm feeling dizzy and sick and put it down to my nerves and all the coffee. What are the chances in

Hell?

It's when I realise I can't face my morning milky coffee, even the smell of coffee actually makes me run to the bathroom to vomit that I realise Hell could have a fighting chance. I'm a bit more emotional than usual, but doing well at hiding it and my body is all sensitive to touch. I feel brittle and scratchy but I don't let it show. I don't dare to say anything to István. I've been in his apartment for over two months since I got back from the frozen north. Unbelievable for us. And I don't want to do anything to risk any arguments. I am so terrified of losing the love of my life. He has been kind, gentle and we haven't fallen out once. If he's been a bit snappy when he's tired, I leave him alone and he is better. I have learned not to take it personally if he has had a stressful day. My shrink has told me he is just using me for sex, and when he has had enough, I will be out of the door. I immediately change my shrink. Nothing is going to burst my István bubble.

But one morning when he brings me coffee in bed, I know I am going to throw up as usual. He goes to the bathroom so I make it to the window and throw up as quietly as I can over someone else's car below. They're going to be mad. I hope they don't know it was me so I close the window. I need to lie down.

It must be a virus, a stomach flu. *Must be something I ate.* I think of the crispy seaweed from last night and feel the nausea rising again. I'm lying to myself. My skirts are feeling a bit tight round the middle but then I have eaten properly since I've been back here.

"Don't you want your coffee, baby?" he asks when he sees me sitting there, the mug untouched.

I say I am feeling sick, must be something I ate. He

looks at me and sits on the bed.

"When was your last period?"

"I don't know," I tell him and he knows this too.

I can't look at him. I cover my face and cry. I tell him, *I have been throwing up every morning and I am afraid I am dying. I am scared it is cancer as I am so sick.*

He laughs and tells me "Sweetheart, you are not dying but I think you might be pregnant. You need to get a test." He says it gently patting my arm. "Go and buy one now. We need to find out."

He's not angry, just matter of fact. He says, *he will call me later.*

I hope he isn't going to kick me out. Maybe the last shrink was right after all. Maybe he will throw me out.

It's a warm May day, just like any other. But I haven't needed to do this before. I am shaking as I buy two different kits from the pharmacy and crying thinking of how angry he is going to be, the thought of him telling me to get out, it isn't his problem. I am thinking the worst. Or what about what he said before he just wanted a child and then I could leave. I feel whatever, he is going to throw me out.

I am shaking as I go back to the apartment and István is in work and I do them both at the same time.

The results are both the same. **Terhes.** One even gives the number of weeks. How does it know that? It is two and a half months. How can I have been like this and not know it?

I am in shock. I sit on the balcony and leave the kits in the bathroom. I go back five minutes later and they haven't changed; that word which changes everything marked out in blue on both. This alone makes me

*throw up. This is totally different from the two
miscarriages I had as I had no idea until it was over
so it wasn't real. This is real and I am afraid things
will go wrong again.*

*I wonder if I should just pack my suitcase and run
now.*

István calls me and asks me, *am I feeling better. Is
there any good news?*

"Nem," I say.

"Oh," he says. He sounds disappointed.

"Terhes vagyok," I can't even say it in English.

"Really?" he says. "I'm so happy." He isn't kidding.
I can hear the smile in his voice. "This is great."

"Please don't tell anyone," I say.

No of course not, he agrees. *But I don't sound very
happy? Why not?*

I'm in shock, I tell him. *I thought I was too thin.*

I tell him, *one of the kits calculates the number of
weeks, there is no need to be jealous. There is no one
else. I have been away but there was no one else.*

He tells me, *he wouldn't doubt it for a minute and
he will be home for lunch break, I need to eat much
more now.*

Lunch break? Has he ever taken a lunch break in
his life?

He is unlocking the door and I go to meet him
unable to look up.

He asks me, *to look at him. See how happy you
made me,* he says. *See how much I want this.*

"I'm sorry," I am crying. "I'm so sorry."

"Hey," he says. "Everything will be alright, I
promise you. I give you my word. It will be so good for
you, you'll see. It will be so good for you to have a kid.
It will all work out great, I know it."

He is full of smiles and I am a nervous wreck. I've

been taking all these fucking sleeping pills and anti-depressants. I drank wine in Lithuania and Latvia. All my clothes are tiny and they're not going to fit. I wasn't imagining this skirt feeling tight. My stomach is swollen already. All those size zero clothes are going to be stuck in the wardrobe. All these thoughts give me a panic attack.

He guesses my thoughts. "We can check everything is okay, you can come off your pills slowly. It won't have done any damage, you've not had alcohol. Don't worry. Please don't worry. You look so unhappy....And please don't be afraid of buying looser clothes. Size zero is not healthy, darling."

I am just terrified. I cannot face another miscarriage either. I will lose my mind.

He promises that I am taking care now and it will be okay this time.

He's chattering away on the balcony as he eats. He doesn't seem like the same István. Where are the terrible arguments or is he just a sleeping volcano? He's telling me the third bedroom is going to be perfect, just the right size for a kid. This is the last reaction I expected from him; excitement and genuine happiness as if I have done something right for once; I have finally given him his heir to the throne, King István.

I can't even think about it. I leave the balcony and go and throw up again. My body is protesting against this alien invasion trying to take refuge in my insides. He comes and sits next to me as I am sitting on the bathroom floor my head spinning. He passes me a glass of water and says he is not going back to work today.

"You what; you are cancelling work?"

"Don't you want me here?" he says looking

wounded.

Of course I do, but I don't want him to miss work on account of me and my mistakes.

I am never a mistake, he tells me. *This is not a mistake, this is meant to happen,* he says with absolute conviction. ***This is us forever.***

It is Friday and he has no more patients only paperwork and he is the boss. *I can do what I want,* he tells me firmly. *I am the boss.* He might as well add, 'of you too, darling.' His ownership of me is complete. He is satisfied.

He sits and looks at the wall and I cannot tell what he is thinking. He has that blank look in his eyes where he seems to be missing for a while, like the shell of him is there and it scares me. *Floating shark,* I think.

"This is us forever," he repeats.

His eyes are completely black and this time I know I am in the fortress looking out, the razor wire wrapping itself around me in a tight circle; his heart.

What have I got myself into?

He is back, the softness in his eyes, helping me up from the bathroom floor asking me, *am I okay, do I need anything?* He can't do enough for me.

Now we have to get married and you will be mine, he says. He is happy about this, like he just won a prize everyone else wanted. He takes me gently to the bedroom and closes the curtains.

No biting, no vampire today just him so kind and loving telling me I am his world. I taste his skin and hair and think of drowning. Sweet flesh, he always tastes so sweet like papaya and passion fruit.

He is so happy all weekend. I am still uncertain about all this but I don't say anything. It is good to see him so relaxed.

It is another few weeks before I dare to get on the scales. My God. I have gained 5 kilos. I can't hold my stomach in and in the bathroom mirror, its swell is noticeable. It is official. My size zero jeans only fit undone. My tiny skirts which were hanging off me as I'd got so thin now cling to my stomach and I can't fasten the zips. My lingerie is all tight. This is the only thing I am happy about. My cleavage looks like I have had plastic surgery but it's swollen and painful to touch. I don't know whether to be happy that I haven't had another miscarriage or scared to death that this kid might be hanging on in there for good.

I'm having to see a shrink as this changing body shape is freaking me out. I am terrified and no one else can really notice it yet. I've been told I look well, I am looking healthy, that I have gained weight and I was way too thin before but I am so afraid, so afraid of getting bigger and bigger until by December I will be like a cow. My only consolation is that it is now June and I can hide my shape when the weather gets cold with my fur coat. I can't imagine if I had ended up this way in winter with all that weight to come in 40c heat. Horrendous.

I wake up every morning and crawl to the bathroom to throw up but then I am okay. I am suddenly hungry. I have to eat.

István is happy for once that he isn't making me eat or worrying about me throwing up deliberately. I have stopped all that. I can't prevent myself from eating. My body is craving fruit and vegetables and everything healthy. It won't let me starve myself.

All the health checks come back clear as they can see and the morning sickness suddenly stops and I am hungry all the time. Everything is normal. I am so relieved that I lose some of my worry. I thought of all those pills I was taking and was sure I would have damaged anything trying to live in my body. Now I am off my pills. I am feeling pretty good. But I am afraid to look at myself in the mirror. My brain still won't process the information. I don't care for the sonogram copy they give me but he does and he keeps looking at it and saying it is beautiful. To me it is evidence of nothing, this ghost grey image they say is a girl. It is July and it is so oppressively hot and I am so conscious that I can't wear any fewer clothes. But I just look nice and healthy, everyone tells me. They can't see I am scared as Hell. I am in the prison of my own skin. I want to leave it and fly away like I did in my dreams. I am afraid as now I am already responsible for everything I do. Everything I put into my body and this is terrifying.

PÓK HÁLÓ

I am standing in my wedding dress, beautiful brilliant red. I am hardly pure but what does it matter which colour as I can't get married alone. Well alone apart from this mini-István which has taken residence inside me and is starting to stretch my skin in a way I cannot stand and is making me feel tight around the middle. There is no István. I am totally alone and humiliated. It is 2pm and it was scheduled for 1pm. I am so angry. I march through the streets, across the square getting strange looks on account of my hair piled up full of diamonds, this brilliant red frock and I am stupid for believing him and I go straight to the dental surgery. No way am I sitting at home waiting hours going out of my mind, or trying to call him. How could I believe he had changed?

No more darkness? This is as dark as it gets. Standing alone on your wedding day.

The receptionist sees me as I walk into the cool green shell of the building and says "Kiára, you look so pretty but what's wrong? What's he done now?"

This is usually what people ask.

"Where is he?" I can't keep my voice down. István comes hurrying out of a treatment room pulling off his gloves and mask.

He sees me and my dress holding a bunch of flowers and his eyes grow wide with fear. He knows what he just forgot. I take the flowers and whack him over the head screaming that I hate him, never want to see him again now I know how little I mean to him.

This is it, I am screaming. *I am leaving you for good. No one does that to me. No one!*

I head out of the door and he chases me grabbing my arm "I am so sorry, I ....."

"Save it, István, I am leaving you now. As soon as it takes to pack a suitcase," I say and I walk into the hot air outside. He drops to his knees and wraps himself around my legs.

"Get off me!" I am trying to push him away. I can't move as he is hanging on so tight.

"Forgive me, forgive me, I lost track of time....I ...I...."

"You fucking idiot!" I scream. "No Versace dress, no cake, no guests, no nothing because all I wanted was you only you weren't there! How many bitches want just that? How many would just be satisfied with their husband and no other money spent? I hate you so much, get off me!"

He is hanging on to me and I can't move and he is sobbing and begging me to forgive him, he will go into the office now and get the next available slot, only first he just has to finish a patient and their implants......

"I'm leaving you, I hate you forever!" I have lost it now and I am crying and screaming. The street is fairly empty but a crowd has gathered in the distance watching this impromptu bit of theatre.

He scoops me up and carries me back inside. I have gone weak now and I am crying like there is no tomorrow. I am so ashamed. He orders one of the assistants to sit with me in the kitchen and get me a coffee and call him immediately if I try to leave. I am not to leave as he knows I will run away again, this time maybe forever. He has another hour and half of surgery to do.

The practice manager comes in to find out what all the shouting is about.

I tell her *I am so sorry, I couldn't sit at home and go out of my mind.*

"The fucking idiot," she says. "The fucking idiot." She is angry on my behalf. All the girls are angry.

The dental assistant who has to watch me agrees. They bring me some chocolates and a coffee.

I ask *does someone have a valium?*

"But should you really take it?" The assistant asks as she fetches one.

"In my condition? It's either that or jump off a building," I say swallowing the pill.

She pats my hand and sits back at the table.

She obviously knows. I am angry as I told him not to tell people too early as I am afraid it will ruin my luck and everything will fall apart.

By the time he comes back I am half asleep across some chairs in the kitchen.

"Has she taken something? Did you give her something? You know she can't take pills in her condition!" he shouts at the poor assistant.

"No, she didn't give it to me. I took it myself," I lie. I don't want to get her into trouble.

"Always have a stash," I murmur sleepily. "It's either that or jumping off the TV tower, which would you prefer?" I ask him.

He gets changed. He is taking me home. Someone else will be finishing the day. He knows he has really fucked up. He carries me out and into his car.

"Some wedding night," I cry into the pillow as he puts me into bed. "It feels like a funeral with all these flowers, with everything you've done." There are so many flowers all over the apartment, their sickly sweet scent in the hot July air is making me feel ill. It does look a bit like someone died. I hurl one of the vases at the wall, shattering its glass and dropping roses everywhere.

"Next week I promise it will be different," he says

his face full of pain. Pain he has caused.

"Yeah, if you remember to turn up. Lucky for you they had a cancellation. Maybe you weren't lying when you said you only wanted a kid and not me."

I picture the mirror as a gravestone **IN LOVING MEMORY OF KIÁRA ÁRGENTA.**

He tries to get into the bed to comfort me. "No!" I scream. "You are crazy! Tonight you can sleep on your own, I can't stand this. What is wrong with you?"

I scratch his face hard and leave claw marks on his lovely skin. He yelps and jumps back as though I am a wild cat. Which today I am. "Get out!" I yell at him trying to swipe my claws at him again.

He puts his head in his hands and says "I'm so sorry, I'm so sorry... Please let me get you something to eat, it's only five, you need to eat."

Be careful what you wish for.

"Fuck off," I say turning over and putting the pillow over my head to close out the beautiful sunlight.

He is crying as he closes the curtains. He kisses the side of my face and I push him away with my eyes still shut. I get up when he leaves the room and rearrange the flowers into unlucky even numbers, as is used for funerals in Hungary. I make the roses I pick up from the floor into unlucky 13 and put the vase by his side of the bed and almost smile.

I am asleep when he comes in around nine, my mascara spidered over my face.

"Love of my life," he says. "I am a stupid, stupid animal, please at least drink your milkshake, I made it for you, it will give you energy." He sets down the milkshake next to the bed.

I don't say anything, I don't know what to say. I sit up and drink the milkshake. I will always drink milk.

It tastes of almonds. That is the taste of cyanide; bitter almonds although if you can smell the almonds it is already too late. I don't care if it is cyanide, in fact I hope it is.

He looks at the flowers next to his night lamp and sighs and takes one out and places it in another vase.

His face is bleeding from my nails, where I scratched him earlier.

"Please forgive me," he slides in next to me. "Please forgive me, I will die if you don't."

I just wrap him in my arms and he falls asleep, his head on my chest. He has been crying a lot, his face is salty. I am still wearing my wedding dress.

I wake up and he is sitting up in bed clutching his left side and his arm.

Oh, Fuck. I have given him a heart attack.

"It's my stomach," he says. "Or maybe it is my heart. I am dying. Help me!"

I am calling an ambulance and he stops me, "No just wait."

He tells me to call his doctor friend, he doesn't want an ambulance.

So I dial Zsolt's number and say *I am sorry it is midnight but István thinks he is having a heart attack.* Zsolt is awake, he is a doctor and an old friend and he says he will be right there.

I am worried sick. I am stroking István's hair and telling him everything is okay, I am sorry for earlier. He is looking so pale and clammy. Now I am feeling guilty for the day as if it is all my fault.

Zsolt is looking at István, checking his heart and breathing so I go and make him a cup of tea as maybe he needs to be alone.

As I am bringing his cup to him, Zsolt is leaving. He tells me there is nothing wrong with István's heart except he doesn't know how to love without hurting. He tells me he is putting it on to get my attention. He doesn't waste any words.

"He is as healthy as anything, Kiára. He needs a shrink, not a doctor. But don't worry about his heart. You need to look after yourself and the baby now. And he needs to look after you."

He hands me a bottle of valium. It is for István in case he has this anxiety attack again. I look at the pills and instantly want to swallow them.

I thank Zsolt and shut the front door.

I am angry István has already told someone, angry he put this act on and frightened me.

"Why did you tell him about me and the kid? First you tell your dental assistant and now him, I told you not to!" I shout at István.

He is sitting up in bed and looking absolutely fine. *Oh, you're fine now,* I think.

He sees the cup of tea I made for Zsolt and reaches for it.

"I was happy, I had to tell someone, please don't be angry, baby, please."

"And your heart is fine. It's just not coping well with loving someone, that's all," I say.

I am so mad as he sits there drinking the tea, calm as anything.

I turn away from him. I can't look at him right now. He tries to hold me. I push him away and sleep as far as I can on the edge of the bed.

When I wake up he is wrapped around me so tight I can hardly breathe. He is in one of his bad dreams again. I have to put the light on and tell him it is okay, I am here. I am not going anywhere, and I think about how fucked up we both are until I can fall asleep again. I have to sit up with him sleeping on my chest so I can hold him and stroke his hair. Why does he have these bad dreams? He won't tell me what they are about.

He glares at me on the way to the registry office the next week. "What's wrong?" I ask him.

He looks like he did when I first met him; devastatingly handsome in his Gucci black and arrogant.

There is a flicker of danger in his eyes when he says "Nothing," and smiles like a cobra ready to strike.

Afterwards, we are heading back to the apartment in the warm sunlight and he laughs in a nasty way and says, *it suits me, slut red.*

I am hardly pure, especially not now, he says as he feels my stomach through the dress. I try to move away, I don't want to be reminded of that stomach.

He's stolen my purity, he goes on. *I am his whore. He laughs some more.*

You cruel bastard, I think. He didn't say it to be funny. Then I remember red makes him mad. I should have chosen black. Funeral black. Red didn't make him mad last week when he missed the wedding and I went mad instead. What is it with red?

I walk on faster, ahead of him. I can't believe he just said that.

He grabs my arm and says "Come on baby, I'm letting you have a glass of champagne tonight. Loosen up."

His eyes have the look of sarcasm in them. He lifts me up and carries me down the street; his prize, for once enjoying the young men looking as they pass on their way out for the evening to bars and restaurants. **Mine,** he whispers into my neck as I unlock our front door.

I wonder what and who the hell I have committed myself to for the rest of my life.

We sit on the balcony. *You're all mine now,* he says more to himself than me. *All mine.*

He looks at the gold band on his hand with pride. I look at the matching one on me and I wonder what took him so long to commit to anyone? He tells me he was so absorbed in his work and he never found the right person. *No one challenged him like me, no one was so free and told him so many times they were just off to work in another country.* He says, *he met his match in me. And I am the most beautiful woman he has ever seen in his life. That was the first thought that came into his head when he first met me.*

Well, that's nice, I think.

Now he has captured me forever. The word 'forever' stretches out into infinity. *You are mine forever. Into infinity and beyond.*

A huge yellow moon hangs low in the sky.

He looks at me. "You will always be mine. I don't want anyone else to touch you. Ever. I mean that, I will not let anyone touch you as you are mine."

His controlling nature which had been in remission has cast an enormous spider web over me. He looks at me without emotion. There is something in his blank look which is so sinister. At this moment I wonder if I truly know this István. All those times I ran away across Europe leaving him the past two years has brought me back full circle.

I look at the stars. ***Be careful what you wish for.***

I realise my work and career have slowly disappeared. István has become my life.

I never see friends or family. I never do anything that doesn't involve him.

He leans over and carries me tenderly inside. Then

his eyes go wild and he rips my red dress saying, *he is going to have me as much as he wants now. I am his property.*

He has only drunk 2 glasses of champagne and it has unleashed the inner animal. It's the only night I really want to stop and I ask him to stop but he is a man possessed.

He tells me, *isn't this what a wedding night is about?* He bites the back of my neck so hard I can taste the blood in his kisses.

I have never seen him like this. He won't stop. When I think he's falling asleep he tears at my dress some more and starts again. The full moon has turned him into a demonic new husband.

I will never wear goddamn red again.

Next morning is Saturday and he keeps saying sorry and he keeps telling me how much he loves me just a little too much to be normal. He is full of remorse for Friday's wedding night. He is obsessed with me. We sit in the park above the city, in Tettye. *Promise me you'll never leave me,* he says wrapping his wedding hand around mine and holding the gold and diamond of my rings up to the dying light.

I try to sit up and he pulls me back down. "We only got married on Friday and I think you consummated it a thousand times since then," I tell him. It's supposed to be funny but he never gets my humour.

He looks at me hurt.

"I promise you, I'll never leave you," I say. I mean it but I can't help worrying about the future. He has unravelled quite a lot this year, not to mention me. But we're trying to pretend it's all going to be okay.

I realise there is one thing we just don't do much of, never have done. And that is laugh. I can't get the Hungarian sense of humour even when I speak the language and he never gets mine. However many radiant smiles a dentist can give you, it is difficult not sharing humour.

He is trying his best to be all light and sweetness and he asks me to choose some pretty toys and a crib for the nursery but I am afraid, think it is tempting fate. It is still too early. If I look forward to it everything might go wrong. I asked my friend to just paint the walls pale pink and put a mirror with pink fluffy heart lights on the wall and some pink curtains.

Where are the toys? István wants to know. *Right now it just looks like a tart's boudoir,* he says.

I ordered a crib and that's it but that would have to go in our room first of all. The room is bare other than this. This empty crib in a bare room.

I tell him, *I can't face doing any more, it's tempting fate. I am afraid something will happen.*

He doesn't understand but says, *okay we can order them later.*

"And nothing bad will happen," he says almost angrily. He stares at me. "Don't even think it, this is mine, don't dare ruin it for me."

This is mine, he is still saying as we are falling asleep, *mine.* He is squeezing me so tight round my middle I feel like a dog toy. I have nightmares that I am mauled by a giant black dog, it is biting my hands off and I wake up with a shock. István doesn't even stir. His black hair is in my mouth and his head is on my chest making it hard to breathe; my new husband. His hands are hanging on to me so tight I wonder if he is dreaming of climbing a cliff face. I might as well be tied to the bed. He must be having one of his bad dreams as he is talking and telling someone, *to stop, **please stop.***

"It's okay," I whisper to him. "I am here, you are

safe with me."

István desperately wants me to go with him to France for three weeks but I can't face it. It will be just as hot and he'll be busy with work and I'll be wandering around on my own. In the end I give in as I think I might start the something that is prickling at the back of my mind. I am afraid not that he will cheat but that I will be convinced he will be cheating and the thought will drive me crazy when I am in this state and I might say or do something I might regret. He also doesn't speak any French and I know he would prefer me there as his translator. He insists I can't stay on my own for three weeks and he doesn't want to spend three weeks without me.

Maybe he is right.

He comes home happy the day before we are due to go to Paris and he has a bag full of soft toys.

"Look what I got," he sings. "Everyone in work bought them for us. For our daughter."

I told him not to tell people. What if something bad happens?

He is busy putting them in the nursery, hanging up a wind chime and placing the toys on the shelves. He has books for a little girl, everything stereotypical. He lovingly places a plush toy zebra in the crib. His favourite is a big plush octopus with a smile on its orange face. He wants it for himself as he reluctantly leaves it in the room but I know by the way I find him holding it at times he wants the octopus.

I am angry with him. Now everyone knows way too early. *It is my body, I should be the one to tell people*, I think.

I am still afraid something will go wrong and I will be left looking at this empty room with the fucking toys and windchime of butterflies.

I have made up my mind, if something goes wrong I will leave. I don't want to be sad looking into this room every day. This is an awful thought with no care for him. I will take my grief and pain and leave him, even though I know it would destroy him. I know as I watch him happily spinning the butterfly windchime it would kill him. He would crash his car into a motorway bridge.

I know there is such a fine line between happiness and total desolation. There is no middle ground for him, or for me. We are either in Heaven with love or we are in Hell. My shrink tells me this is the bipolar condition and that the meds are supposed to control that only I can't take my meds right now and he refuses to consider himself bipolar so he won't even take a single pill. So where does that leave us? Burning in passion or burning in pain.

PÁRIZS ŐRÜLTSÉG

Paris is horrible. I had forgotten how much I disliked the place. Sleazy and hot. Noisy and dirty. Despite it being on my passport as my birthplace, Paris and I do not like each other. I associate it with straggly cords of beggars following me around when I was a teenager and pimps trying to buy me on the metro. I took up smoking in Paris when I was 16 as I spent a whole miserable summer in the suburbs with a sullen French friend and her family. I never saw Paris as a beautiful romantic place. There is no beauty in Paris compared to Budapest. It is full of rip-offs and misery. This was a mistake. I should have called Katalin and gone up to Tihany on Lake Balaton with her and some friends. They had invited me. She is worried I am living my life dictated by István. She is right and I shouldn't be neurotic about not being thin enough for a bikini. She dislikes him so much she doesn't visit when he is around. She won't expand on this but says he has a reputation. *He is a woman-hater,* she has more or less said.

I should also feel more empowered as my French always has even the Parisians polite and welcoming. We are staying near the Champs Elysées and we are high up with a balcony. It should be nice. Well, it would if it were for a week and I wasn't alone 12 hours a day.

The manager in the hotel likes us and in the expensive restaurant István chooses I should feel happy that I am the one in command of the language. His French is hopeless, he doesn't notice I have ordered a small glass of wine and he is angry when it arrives along with his large glass of red. We argue about the wine so I ask the waiter how many pregnant French women drink a small amount twice a week. He tells me it's fairly usual. This puts Mister into a sulk all through dinner. But I don't feel good. I don't feel good at all. These dental conferences go on late into the evening. When he returns he is hungry. And when he has eaten he needs his fill of me. This is all there is for me in Paris; dinner and sex. He is not talking much, he lets me order dinner and then we eat in virtual silence and then he is physically demanding. It's as though neither of us is speaking the other's language. I am speaking French and this makes him silent, he doesn't want to talk about his day; *he is tired. He only wants to eat and fuck.*

He says this one evening when I am asking about his day.

"Baby, I am tired okay? I just want to eat and then fuck."

He doesn't even look up from his foie gras. He is stuffing his face and then he wants to stuff me too.

I say this and he doesn't even respond. It was meant to be funny but he never gets my humour anyway. Aside from teeth, the only things he enjoys are eating and fucking. He never watches films with me, he hates all those French and Italian ones I love. He never reads unless it is about dentistry. He plays some sport twice a week, but without enjoyment, just to stay healthy. He travels only for conferences. He dislikes beaches, art, holidays, relaxing, anything I mention. I am the centre of his universe and I come second to dentistry. He is one-dimensional. Or maybe the obsessions in his life took over and squashed everything else out. I still am not convinced it is love for me in his heart, purely obsession.

It's only the fifth day we are there and around 7pm

after a conference, István calls to say he will be a bit later, he's got to go with some colleagues to a bar to talk things over. *They covered a lot of new areas today and it's important and one of the men has an auntie with a complicated dental problem which is in his area of expertise, he might need to see her.*

Okay. Credible enough, I think.

It gets to ten at night. I try his phone. It is switched off. He's not a big drinker although he will drink a little so I know it's not a drinking night out. I don't know if it worse to be here in this situation where the dark hot and sinister streets of Paris have swallowed up my man or back in Hungary, going crazy not knowing where he is and why he won't answer. I try to calm my mind, I phone my mother who reassures me everything is okay, he will be back. *Aren't I enjoying seeing Paris again?*

But in my head I see him with another woman, kissing her, getting into her bed. I am losing it. At midnight I go down to the front desk of the hotel and ask for a cigarette lighter so I can smoke on my balcony. The manager is flirty and nice and asks if I want to smoke with him at the front of the building. This makes me feel better. He obviously doesn't notice I'm pregnant.

I thank him but say, *I need to call my family and maybe another time.* Upstairs in the hotel room I go and look at myself in the bathroom mirror. No, it's not obvious unless I pull my loose top up and you can see my stomach is swollen. But it's only five months and as I am so slim, I can hide it. It is still freaking me out. But I cannot hide it with myself as each week the weighing scales are slowly creeping up, the skin on my stomach pushing itself out in a way that makes me afraid. Natalija is already fighting her way into the world, letting me know she is there.

I sit in the cream marbled bathroom. I burn my arm just like I did so many times before. It hurts and I focus on the pain and the hiss of the cigarette lighter. It is now nearly 1am. I try his phone again. *Answerphone; that dead, sick emptiness of space. The absence of the person you always want to talk to most in the whole world.* I want to take my emergency valium, I need a drink but I can't. I'm afraid to take drugs since I can't forgive myself if I damage this kid. I am burning the pain away and I reason that it is calming me down and preventing my stress levels shooting through the roof. I'm afraid of getting so angry and having a miscarriage. I can't stop the flames of rage which are starting to get out of control. I know I will do something terrible if I sit in this hotel room. I have to get out. I have to leave him now. I can't believe he has done this to me when I am vulnerable, especially after last week. I get my handbag, stuff in my passport and a change of clothes. I disappear into the sullen night sky. The manager doesn't see. His head is bent over his books.

I wait on the road outside, the dirty breath of the hated city wrapping me in its vile shroud, until some other hotel guests arrive back in a taxi. I ask the driver can he take me *to* Paris Austerlitz. *Of course,* he says. *Anywhere for such a beautiful lady. Are you married?*

I smile and tell him, *I am happily married and have a kid.* Why is it at my most vulnerable I have a radar which attracts all men from the age of 14 to 90?

He says, *my husband is the luckiest man in the world.*

I thank him. He doesn't know the truth. I am such a good liar. Maybe I learned to lie in journalism school. After all you write about murder trials and cases you don't agree with but give out what you are told in work. *Guilty? No, of course not, he is innocent.* This paedophile triple axe murderer.

I am burning with rage and I have to do something. I am there at 4am and there is a 5am departure to the south. I can get to my relatives who live near Bordeaux. My phone is ringing and ringing. I look at the display. István. It rings about five times.

I call my mother again who is woken up and I say, *I'm okay, but I need to get to my uncle's house. I can't stay with István.*

She is telling me, *she is sure there is a good explanation.*

No, no, no, I am shouting down the phone.

She says, *that she will call my uncle at 8am and let him know, he will be there but she can't call now. He'll think it's an emergency.*

Hell. This is a fucking emergency.

There is a voicemail from István, "Baby, where are you? I've been trying to call. I'm really sorry. Please answer. I'm in the hotel. I can explain everything. It isn't what you think." His voice is shaking.

Yeah, yeah. That means it is what I think. I think I would have gone as crazy as I have gone in my life if I had been in that hotel room and he arrived back at 4am covered in perfume. Crazy.

I put the phone on silent. I have another 10 missed calls and three more voicemails.

He is pleading with me to call him, let him know what happened. Am I in hospital? Has something happened? He's frightened.

I realise I can't let him think that I've had a miscarriage or anything. That isn't fair. I should have just told the manager to tell him I'd gone out for a walk.

I text. ***I am okay. Without you. I hate you.***

I get on the train. He has texted me back. ***Szeretlek. Hol vagy? Kedvesem.***

So now he is worried, now he loves me. I can't be in this powerless position.

But the urge to answer the phone just gets the better of me. I have to speak Hungarian as I just can't have this train carriage of people eating breakfast knowing my life. Not that they'll see me again.

The TGV bullets out of Paris heading south. I loved this journey once, seeing the buildings and landscape morph into sweeter versions of themselves heading south but I am not resting too easy on this journey. I need at least 15mg of valium which I can't take. I even feel guilty for the coffee I have in the morning. This is not me. I was once the party girl who passed out with a bottle on her bed every night at university and still ended up with a first class honours degree. And sometimes it was vodka, not wine, especially in my year out in Latvia. Wine was too expensive there. It was waking up to an empty bottle of vodka and knowing I had to head to the lecture theatre or the newspaper despite the killer hangover. But I would always go unless I was throwing up so much I couldn't move as to get out and about is the best thing for depression and a hangover and then makes drinking the next day more fun.

Maybe that was not so healthy. I am healthier now, I look healthier and I am less depressed. Alcohol is not a mood elevator, that's clear. I have improved. I am not a drunken journalist any longer.

I dial Mister's number and he answers on the first ring, frantic. I tell him I have gone out.

"Where were you, István? Who were you fucking?

You turned your phone off and fucked someone, didn't you? Don't I give you enough? I haven't missed a night and you know it! Do I ever say I can't, I've got a headache?? Do I?" I am so right and he knows it.

"Baby, please listen to me, please stop swearing. I would never ever do that to you. I swear on my life. My colleague, his relative had a dental emergency and I......"

"You have got to be kidding me", I tell him. "You think I am buying that??? At four in the fucking morning you had a dental emergency?"

"Please, this auntie of my friend, she needed surgery. It was so complex, I lost track of time. I am so, so stupid. Please just come back," he pleads.

"I can't. Never and you will never see your child, István."

"How can you say this to me? How can you say that?" He is actually crying on the phone. "Darling, I am begging you to come back. I have never begged anyone to come back to me in my life. Don't say I will never see my kid! You will regret it for the rest of your life and I will die, I'll die because my heart would break! And your heart will break without me, I know you too well now."

I think mine would too, he is right. I don't know why I threaten this when I know there is no way I could even contemplate it, whatever monster István turned into. And I could never say he is a monster, just hopelessly involved in his work, messed up, insecure and just plain strange. To live without him would to be living in a world without colour, just oxygen, a grey sky and no violent palettes of colour whether good or bad. *I love him so much my heart could break.*

Well he is stupid enough about his work to lose

complete track of time. The day we were supposed to get married in July, the first time he forgot to show up leaving me standing there in my wedding dress. Nothing burned more than that. He fucking forgot. I haven't forgiven him for that.

"You never married me that first time because you forgot. You fucking forgot when all I wanted was some cheap register office, just you, no cake, no friends, no Versace dress. Fuck you!"

"Baby tell me where you are. Tell me, I promise. That was awful for you I know, but didn't I book the wedding the next week? Didn't I?"

I want to tell him to stay in Hell.

I am already there.

"I'm on the Bordeaux train. I'm going to my uncle's house."

"Kiára, my darling Kiára, my heart is breaking. One night without you is Hell," he is sobbing into my phone so loud, I think people can hear.

"Well I just spent a night without you, not knowing where the Hell you were!"

"I'm coming to get you back; I'm coming down to your uncle's. I beg you not to hurt yourself or the child," he is desperate as he chokes on his tears.

"Too late for that," I say.

"No!" he is screaming down the phone. "No! What have you done to my baby? I'll die if you've hurt her!"

"Oh calm down. It was only me. The kid is fine."

"Kiára, what did you do to yourself? Did you self-harm? Oh, God, I'm taking the next train after you. Promise me you won't do anything else bad, promise?"

"I promise. Good luck finding me," I say.

I hang up.

He tries calling me back a few times. He says on the last voicemail, *he will call my mother in Wales at*

8am to get my uncle's address in south-west France. It's too early now. He tells me *he loves me more than life itself.*

This is the problem. We both do. I love him more than life itself too.

The older woman across the aisle from me leans over and pats my arm.

"Sajnálom, drágám."

Oh fuck me. What are the chances of a Hungarian on the early morning train to Bordeaux? She brings me a breakfast from the buffet car when she gets hers. She is going to see her daughter who lives in France. I thank her. István is right. I have to stop this swearing.

I get out of the train and my uncle is happy to see me. In the car I tell him, *I'm sorry but I had a bit of a domestic.*

He asks, *is everything okay? Where is my man?*

I tell him, *he might be on his way.*

He's fine with this. *No problem. There's food and wine in the kitchen, stay some days if you like, or both of you. Just relax and look at the sunflowers.*

He puts a chair for me under the Judas tree. Isn't that where the unfaithful hang themselves?

That would be fitting.

I'm sitting by the poolside in the middle of nowhere. This is only a hamlet in Cognac region. It's heading later into the afternoon and I wonder if István will bother turning up at all. If he doesn't, I have decided I will leave him and never go back. I still can't sleep. I can't think straight. My uncle cleans the swimming pool in case I would like to swim. My thoughts are racing and Amandine next door is talking to her rooster and chickens.

You, Monsieur, you took such a big mouthful, there

won't be any left for the girls.

Everyone is nuts. My life is nuts. I will end up like Amandine, talking to my chickens.

I take off my dress and flop into the swimming pool in my underwear and float for a bit looking at the perfect azure of the sky. I swim a little and then get out and lie in the sun.

I can't sleep despite being so tired and the sunflowers waving their heavy heads at me. I'm trying to calm down but it isn't working. I am still afraid István cheated on me.

My uncle brings me a pineau aperitif as he is preparing escargots for dinner for later as he knows they are my favourite. Sometime soon after, a taxi pulls up in the dirt road and my uncle goes to open the gate. István looks kind of strange here in this quiet French backwater in his black designer suit in this heat. His black curls are wild and uncombed and he has a crazy look about him. He obviously called my mother to find this place. He sees me and runs to me. For a minute I am afraid of what he's going to do. His eyes are rimmed red with crying. He drops to the floor and says "Forgive me, please forgive me or I'll die." He puts his head on my stomach and cries. He sees my burnt arm and cries harder. "Oh God. What did you do to yourself? It's all my fault."

I'm crying too and holding him so tight. "I'm sorry, I'm really sorry."

There's no perfume on him, not a trace just his skin smell, his hair. He hasn't showered, he hasn't slept.

SMARAGD- A SZÍN IRIGYSÉG

We are lying in bed in my uncle's farmhouse. Lucky my relatives are so understanding. They must think I found myself a really strange Hungarian but they know I wouldn't be with someone dull.

István is sleeping his body wrapped so tight around me as if I might run away in the night. He swallowed the dinner of escargots and langoustines and a selection of cheeses with some local red wine hardly speaking but thanked my uncle profusely for his generosity. I need to go to the bathroom but I can't loosen his grip. I look at his black eyelashes, his handsome face and think if I had to live without him I would die, whatever he did last night. No he didn't cheat but if he ever did, I could never leave him, I know that. He feels me trying to move a little and wraps himself tighter, a boa constrictor. He is murmuring in his sleep about teeth and emeralds; *he must get the emeralds to the Queen and is his horse ready for the battle.*

I know he was telling the truth, know how obsessed he becomes when he works. He bought me a huge emerald in Paris to match the diamond ring promising me the world. I know he didn't cheat on me.

I hold my left hand up and look at the emerald and then raise my right hand and look at the diamond from Norway next to the gold wedding ring and they shine so beautifully. *Why is beauty so cruel?* I think looking at him. *You are so cruel.* I touch my stomach. I am full of him, she will be a clone of him; a mini-István. Beautiful and wilful so he will give her everything and spoil her and she will hate me. I will be the one left out. Three is not a good number. He's got me tied to him forever with this kid. I feel angry.

Then I kiss his lips and his eyelashes. He is like a sleeping God; no savage nightmares tonight, he is sleeping well in this country retreat in south-west France despite murmuring about battles and he is the King again. He is soft and says it peacefully, not the distressed shouting he often does.

How can someone so beautiful be so messed up? I am worried for him and his mental health and wonder do we make each other worse or is it better to be with someone who understands madness and loves you unconditionally? I hope he is just imaginative and prone to night terrors. I know he probably has bipolar one, which is more serious, especially as he won't admit to any problems.

My emotions are all over the place. I want to slap him and pull his hair one minute then embrace him the next. I start to worry that he might lose the plot completely and I will end up looking after him as well as a kid. He seems so unstable at the moment. No, more likely it will be me losing the plot as always. His dentistry and surgery anchors him. Just as well he chose medicine and not music or art. I still don't know why he has to buy my love with two enormous rocks. How can you count running through a Norwegian airport as an engagement, then when he forgot to marry me that day last month or this behaviour now?

But then romance has always left me cold. I hate Valentine's Day. I am worried about this as I remember the wedding day, how we had discussed it over breakfast and how he forgot only a few hours' later. I thought at the time it was all because he couldn't care less, now I am more worried about his mental state that he can forget something like that.

I have visions of me dead and him forgetting he has

a kid and leaving it out in the snow or something, remembering two days' later and the little girl has frozen to death on the balcony. In these visions or nightmares I have, I am always dead, looking down on him and our apartment, him and the little girl. I am not part of my future. She is almost not a part of me. I am just a vessel, something to carry her into the world and then my work will be done. These thoughts are so strong.

I am never there and this is sinister. I can't even talk to anyone about it. I am afraid the premonition will come true. I am convinced it means I will die. I am too afraid to voice my worst fears and they just grow and grow.

And they do. They are snapped shut in a locked box, but the box is already starting to rattle and bulge at the edges, so I throw it in an empty room. I don't realise I am only delaying the inevitable by refusing to engage with it. Eventually it will burst from its confines. It is stronger than me.

István calls Paris and says he can't attend the next day but he is planning to take the early train the following morning. He is sitting under the Judas tree in his suit although he showered.

I tell him that's where the unfaithful hang themselves as I bring him a croissant with his juice for breakfast. He looks at me, hurt and puzzled. I drop the croissant into his lap. My uncle brings us some coffee.

You idiot, I think about István.

He's been up for some time thinking. He refuses to borrow shorts from my uncle but agrees to borrow a T-shirt while I wash his shirt. He eventually agrees to take off his hot trousers and flop into the swimming pool and float.

My star, I think. He is looking up at the Heavens and he is star-shaped. I am in pain with this love and hate I feel.

My uncle says, *it is lovely to finally meet this dentist he has heard so much about, he is every bit as handsome as I said. He has lousy teeth himself,* he tells István.

István cannot resist this chance to analyse a new patient. He leaps out of the swimming pool immediately and reclines the sunchair so that he can see into my uncle's mouth. He reels off a list of treatments and problems.

He is not out to make money, he knows my uncle will probably never get himself over to Hungary.

He is just so obsessed with teeth and bones and surgery.

In the white sunlight the emerald is beautiful on my hand. He is worried I don't like it. He says *he wanted the biggest stone he could find but if I don't like it he can take it back.* He is worried the diamond wasn't enough as it didn't make me stay with him. But has he ever given me the choice in what I do?

No, it's beautiful, I tell him. But I am still brittle. He keeps thinking he has to make up for his irrational and sometimes crazy behaviour with expensive jewels, as if I won't love him enough without it.

This last remark is strange. He lowers his eyes. Despite his arrogant front he is a lonely and uncertain man and he knows he is deeply messed up. But he doesn't know I am way more messed up than him really.

He won't shut up over dinner. He loves to charm. He is gabbling away to my uncle who has made a Chinese meal. My fortune cookie says **Be careful what you wish for.**

How fitting, I say sarcastically to István. *How many times have I thought this in the last year?*

His eyes flicker with hurt. He has not seen this side of me for a while.

István's cookie is empty. I laugh just a little too much. It's not really funny but the look on his face is as he is shaking the cookie and the wrapper, looking for his fortune. My uncle has poured me a glass of wine and I can see István's face. He wants to tell him I must not drink in my condition. I had a tiny pineau aperitif yesterday he didn't know about. But he can't tell my uncle not to pour me a small glass of wine as it would be rude to question his authority, this is his house. It's only the second glass in four months I am thinking as he is glaring at me.

"We'll be going back to Paris early tomorrow," he says his mouth full.

My uncle says, *we're more than welcome to stay, plenty of room as my auntie is away.*

I say, *thank you. I will do.*

"But...." István turns to me.

"I am not going back to Paris," I say calmly. "Not tomorrow, not ever."

When we are safe in the separate area of the house, István is angry. That is an understatement. He is mad.

"How could you show me up like that in front of your uncle?"

He has that look of danger I have not seen for a long time. His eyes are full of it.

He grips my arm and says "Look at yourself. Look at what you've done. Self-harming. You disgust me. Drinking in your condition, harming the baby."

His grip is hurting. He accuses me of wanting to go back to Hungary to fuck young men and get drunk every night.

He says, *he is convinced that's why I am going back. It makes him ill thinking of me with someone with his kid inside me.*

He tells me, *I am messed up, running off in the night; his work comes first and I have cost him two days of an important conference and if I go back to Hungary and leave him alone in Paris he will die.*

I tell him, *stop threatening, I can go if I want.*

He says, *if I do that, he will stop me.*

Just try, I say.

He will drag me through the courts in Hungary if he has to, he says. *I am his wife; I belong to him.*

I tell him, *two glasses of wine in four months is not a tragedy. French women do it.*

We say the worst things to each other. He says, *he will kill himself if I don't stay, he will jump into the Seine.*

It is horrible. I accuse him of using me as a sex toy and that's the only reason I am in Paris.

He asks me, *would I rather he went with someone else; there are plenty of beautiful women in Paris?*

He spits out this last remark with such venom the poison goes straight to my heart.

He pins me down on the bed. He is rough, he bites me and I scratch his back as hard as I can with my sharp nails. His eyes have gone black with hate and he holds both my arms to stop me scratching him to pieces.

The only part of me is gentle with is my jaw. He treats it as sacred due to the damage it had and the constant treatment he has to give it. However wild he can be his kisses are the most gentle I have ever had in my life, his mouth the sweetest. Before him I hated kissing. I am holding this thought until we turn feral again and I want to hurt him so badly and his face is full of rage.

I can't leave him, he is sobbing afterwards. His back looks as though a cat has mauled it and I have purple bites over my back and shoulders. *He's never needed someone so much, I am the most beautiful woman on earth, an angel.* We are both sorry. I can't leave him, however much I am angry with him. I know if I left him, I would leave life itself. I am so afraid for him too; I know he would jump into the Seine. He doesn't make idle threats like some men I have known. He is a Hungarian and he knows and has been touched by suicide and I know he is capable of it. I remember my friend Eszter laughing and saying it was really 'trendy' to jump from the Szabadság Híd. She had climbed it herself when she was drunk and lovesick one night but changed her mind once she reached the top. *The other Budapest bridges are a bit boring, maybe Lánchíd with the stone lions but the Szabadság Híd was the way to go,* she said. I am afraid István will jump from any bridge in Paris right now if I leave.

'We Hungarians are very very good at suicide,' Eszter had told me laughing.

So we go back to goddamn Paris. I can't leave him alone here. I trawl round some modern art galleries, but my heart isn't in it. It's too hot in the city in August. I am scratchy and wish I was somewhere less land-locked.

But he never comes back late again. He is back at 6pm like an enthusiastic puppy lifting me in the air and taking me to dinner, for once keen to talk about his day, wanting to know which gallery I visited during mine. I find out later he has spoken to the hotel manager and ordered him to phone him if he

sees me leaving or if I am out for more than a few
hours at a time. I look in the top drawer one day and I
am shocked to find he has been taking my passport
around with him at all times. He is so serious about
me running away from him. I question him about it
and he tells me my hormones are out of control, he
has to make sure I am safe.

He tells the manager, *I am pregnant and bipolar
and it is very serious. He is my husband and he is my
guardian.* He convinces the hotel staff to call him
immediately after 3 hours. I am not happy he is giving
this information to the hotel staff.

*I am his prisoner. I am under house arrest, or
rather hotel arrest.*

ENYÉM VAGY

We arrive back on the first Friday in September and I know we are both sick. We both need help. His bipolar is surfacing more and more these days and I am struggling with my own demons. His friend has suggested he needs to see a shrink but he denies he has any problems.

Life is just great, he says. Zsolt his doctor friend has urged me to get him help; he hopes I can persuade him. He says that István is a childhood friend and they went to university together in Szeged and he knows how badly he was affected by his parents' sudden death but refused to talk, he lost himself in work more and more. Zsolt is desperate that nothing jeopardises my marriage to István as he knows that he would never recover if I wasn't there, he knows he has never really loved anyone or trusted them before.

Without wanting to make me feel guilty, Zsolt has told me straight up "If he lost you, Kiára, it would kill him."

Saturday and Sunday István is full of remorse. *He is feeling guilty about so many things,* he says. *About Paris, about cruel words he said to me, about hurting me in bed when he loves me so much.* He brings croissants into the bedroom although he hates breakfast in bed as he says it makes such a mess. He is driving me around to sculpture parks, beautiful vistas, any restaurant I want to go to. He smiles at a little girl in the park and throws her ball back for her and tells me for the hundredth time, *it will be so good for me to have a kid, I won't feel depressed ever again.*

He thinks it is the answer to all my troubles.

She's going to be as beautiful as me, he carries on.

He will have two Kiáras in his life then.

I laugh as this sounds like Humbert in *Lolita;* wanting to reproduce so he can make a clone of her so he can have more satisfaction than he already has.

He is hurt and says, *how can I even think like that? It will be his daughter, he says.*

I am joking, I say. *Did you never read Nabokov? Maybe we could watch the film…….*

She will be pure, he says. *Do I even think for one minute he is capable of molesting his own daughter? No one will touch her. No one. Ever.*

You are sick, he says. *Really sick.*

He is crying and walking out of the park.

"Is that what you think of me?" He wants to know. "Do you think I am some kind of monster, you think I would hurt my little girl? My own flesh and blood? I wouldn't do that to any kid, no one.

And this is my daughter."

Of course I don't think that, but he never finds my humour in the least bit funny. He always takes offence or just looks puzzled.

But I do find it disturbing that he wants her to be a goddamn nun for the rest of her life now. God help her when she wants to start dating.

I have an image of István stopping fourteen year old Natalija going out to a disco and them screaming at each other like Humbert and Lolita, but of course I don't think for a minute István would molest his daughter. I just think he will hate any boy who tries to date her as he is a jealous type. I am never in these visions. I am always looking from above. István is trying to hold her and wipe off her streak of red lipstick as she wrestles away from him, her beautiful dark eyes and long black curls wild. A little Carmen screaming at István "I hate you, I hate you!"

I tell him, *I was kidding.*

Once again he just didn't get my humour.

"Of course I don't think that about you," I tell him.

But the mood is dead. We drive back home in silence. He is silent and his face is wet with tears.

What do I do these days? I never made a man cry so much in my life.

He is now crying about her name on the way home, saying it is not Hungarian enough. There is even a law which means children have to have Hungarian names or at least the spelling has to be Hungarian, unless one parent is foreign, which applies to me. He says it is too Russian, too Latvian. He wanted the name Lilla after his mother but I said I only liked Lilja which he also said was too Russian. So Natalija Enikő it will be. He gives her a Hungarian middle name, just in case. *More like in case he decides to change it if I am dead. What am I talking about? Why do I have this feeling I am not going to be around?*

Some time after, he feels he can go to America for five days for training and leave me but he has taken my passport again. I don't believe it. I call his cell phone and ask him, "we're married, what do you think I'm going to do?"

"Yes," he tells me blankly, that dead look in his eyes although I can't see it I can sense it on the phone. "I have your passport with me right here, my darling wife. Just in case."

Where does he think I am going to run to in my condition? Does he seriously think I am a flight risk?

He sends a never-ending stream of people to check up on me. They say they are here to see me and drink coffee on the balcony and chat. But I know they are here to report back to him about me.

Does he seriously think I am going to cheat on him?

I have nightmares. I dream of this alien growing inside me and I feel such panic when I wake up. I am relieved at least it is a girl so it can't be exactly like him. I think of myself only a year ago climbing over an iron gate in Sicily, light and agile. Now I am heavy, weighed down to earth and it makes me panicky.

He arrives back on the Red-Eye from New York on a Monday and goes straight to work. He comes back that evening tired and grouchy at 9pm. He's been in surgery all day. I go to embrace him at the door and he pushes me away. "Stop it, baby," he says. "I'm really tired."

I am so hurt. He hasn't done this before. Well, not since I have officially been with him this year.

I tell him, *he should eat something.*

"Listen, sweetheart," he jabs his finger into my chest. "You are my wife. You don't tell me what to do. You got that, you got that?!"

He goes into the bedroom. I pick up the car keys and my bag and leave.

He shouts as I am leaving but I carry on.

I am afraid he has been with someone more beautiful in America and it is not me.

It's cool outside, the warm late September is giving way to the night chill, the slide towards winter.

I don't know what to do or where to go. I am just driving around. I park up on the hill near Tettye and sleep. He must be sleeping too because a call at midnight on my cell phone wakes me up. The same frantic sound in his voice, the same desperation.

He's in a taxi up where I'm parked and it's the same shouting, the same anger, then the tears from us both, the same forgiveness, the same love and hate. I tell him, *I was hurt by him pushing me away, scared he was with someone in America.*

He tells me, *he was exhausted, he was dead on his feet with tiredness and he would never ever even dream of another woman.* We are in bed at three am and he is crying quietly. I am crying into the pillow turned away from him. We both need help. He's been rough again and he's hurt me, I have hurt him and scratched his face and I am sorry, he is sorry. It's an addiction. He opens a box from the drawer next to my bed and produces diamond earrings which he carefully fits into my ears. This is his gift from America and then he passes out squeezing me so tight I can hardly move.

Next morning I look for my passport in the apartment. It is not there.

I call the surgery, I can't face going in. He's busy. *He'll call me back,* they say.

This brings back bad memories. The voices in my head are screaming, *Go he doesn't want you!*

The emerald ring on my hand glints a beautiful shade of green envy.

Has he found someone else in America? Didn't he say he had a girlfriend in America once?

He doesn't call me back that day.

I feel frenzied, I want to hurt myself so much.

Katalin is not working so she comes over to stop me going mad. Actually, I don't tell her this. I pretend we are okay. I just need to stop thinking. We are destroying each other with our jealousy.

Maybe this is the end? But my voice of reason is telling me he married me only in July.

I always think everything is the end.

Kata is busy eating with me and we are drinking wine. I tell her, *just one glass.*

At eight that evening, I am laughing at something

Kata has just told me about her latest disaster date when I feel a presence in the doorway. I didn't hear the key.

Kata immediately looks so frightened I think it's a ghost. But no, it's István and he doesn't need to say a word. I can tell the mood he is in. His eyes are black.

Kata says, *she forgot the time, she better go and practically runs out of the door.*

István stands there looking at me with such hatred.

He says slowly "You are drinking again."

One glass. One tiny glass.

He looks at the wine glass in my hand, picks it up and hurls it at the wall.

I am so afraid it brings back memories of the man in Valencia.

I slide off the sofa and onto the floor and say "Don't hurt me. I'm afraid of you."

I cry, wrapping myself into the smallest ball I can.

"I was in a business dinner, I couldn't call you because I was so angry with you, when I had to come up to find you at midnight I thought you were with another man," he says. He is taking off his jacket and belt.

"I was angry with you, you pushed me away when you came back from America, you acted like you hated me and I promise you I was alone last night sleeping in the car and I only drank one glass of wine," I say through tears and hate my vulnerability.

He slides down onto the floor and sits next to me. "I do hate you," he says. "But I love you more than life itself. I've lost control. I've lost myself in you, in your body, your eyes, your hair, your skin. I feel like I'm drowning." He sits there stunned at what he has just admitted to.

180

He carries on "I am a Hungarian man, it's so hard for me to admit all this but I would never hurt you, baby, and I was so tired yesterday, I was grouchy and I shouldn't have been. Did you really think I would hit you like that man did? The man whose damage I am still fixing?"

He is pulling at my dress, his hands creeping up my stocking tops. I look into his eyes and the pupil has dilated to fill the iris giving that black empty look. He is angry and aroused.

"I thought you were with someone in America," I say.

"Never, never ever." His eyes are clear again and honest and hurt. Then they turn black and depthless and he leans over and kisses me pulling at my hair. "I only want you, baby. I thought of you all week. It drove me crazy." But his hands are too rough and he is focussed on what he wants now. He can't see the tears running down my face as he does what he wants with love, passion and hate. He tells me, *he's fantasised about this every night in America, dying for me and my flesh.*

He thinks this is as good for me as it is for him.

And then the usual "Baby, why are you crying? I didn't hurt you did I? Please tell me I didn't hurt you...."

I wonder what happened to me and my life.

BETEGSÉG

We can't deny anything any longer. Our love has turned into raging obsession. We both go to a shrink together. We are so obsessed with each other it has turned into a sickness, we are both afraid. Afraid of the passion and the hate and insane jealousy which goes with it. I am afraid he will cheat, he is afraid I will run away. We walk in holding hands and don't let go until near the end.

The hiding of my passport shocks even the shrink. He says he has not seen a couple so obsessed with each other, so beautiful.

I make a joke we are brother and sister, we have the same blood and now we will have a baby.

This is not funny to anyone but me. I laugh at my own joke. It's not really funny at all but I am finding it hysterical. The shrink is writing away. I can see this **Deteriorating mental condition complicated by bipolar 2. Jokes husband is brother. Husband emotionally unstable and possibly bipolar 1. God help the child.**

István weeps uncontrollably and says *he loves me so much he is afraid of me running away and him never finding me again. He says it would kill him. Work was his life,* he says. *And now I am his life.* He tells the shrink, t*hat he just wants my body so much it kills him, he wants it over and over and over.* He says *he doesn't know he's hurt me until afterwards and he feels like a monster when he knows I haven't enjoyed it, he's almost in another world and he hates himself for being cruel to me.*

The shrink tells him straight "Your wife is vulnerable. You are forcing yourself on her night after night. She needs you to make love to her. Be gentle."

This shrink is a man but he seems to be in favour of me. Maybe because I sit there all delicate with this swell of my stomach; I'm also laughing for no reason at all. I keep finding innuendoes in everything the shrink says and laughing out loud.

István is crying and crying. He told me he never cried in his life until he met me. I don't know if this is good or bad. He is making up for lost time.

I try to say that *no, really, I admit he has hurt me but it doesn't mean we have to go to vanilla sex.......*

Our hour is nearly up.

I have to say something so I tell the shrink about István and his nightmares. The King of Hungary and all the standing at the bedroom window in some kind of sleepwalk calling in the battle; that he refers to me as his Queen and has done ever since he first met me saying he waited a thousand years for me.

István fixes me with a look of such hurt betrayal. I don't look but I feel the intensity of his gaze and he lets go of my hand and hides his face with his hands.

God, I have to tell someone. It is making me ill. Night after night.

The shrink says *we need a lot more help.* He says *he has never seen such a strange situation. He knows I am bipolar and he thinks István is bipolar one, more dangerous and life-threatening than my bipolar two.*

Has he ever tried to kill himself, Kiára? he probes.

I tell him about the car incident that August on Tettye and we could have died.

I tell him, *he has threatened to kill himself several times.*

I tell him about the mood swings which have nothing to do with drink or drugs as he only has a glass of wine or two with food and not even every day and he won't even take prescription drugs for a headache.

István is looking at me like I betrayed him. He is a hurt little boy.

The shrink says, *we are in a serious condition, this has to be dealt with and István should take medication. We have to be stable for the child, we have to think of her. István needs medication.*

I know the answer to that even before he shouts at the shrink, *that he is a doctor too and he doesn't need tablets!*

"You quack!" he shouts as he walks out to pay the bill.

This makes me laugh even more I can hardly get up. I laugh until I am crying and hysterical and the shrink has to help me out of the chair.

I can't control my emotions. I just hope it's hormones and I hope it is influencing István and that we are both going to get better. I hope.

He is angry with me as we leave. *He is the King of Hungary, he is István. He is not bipolar. But he is sick,* he admits.

I tell him "We have to tell the shrink even if we tell no one else. I can't deal with it alone, István. The nightmares, the shouting, the sleepwalking. I love you so much and I will care for you through eternity but I have to tell the shrink. If you refuse meds, it is up to you, but I have to talk. I have told no one about this. And maybe you are right. Maybe you are the King of Hungary, maybe you are the reincarnation of him and I am your Queen but I have to tell the shrink otherwise why are we paying him?"

I am driving him home for once. He can't face it. He has been upset. He can't do anything that night. I virtually have to put him to bed. I make sure the light is as bright as I can stand it for us to sleep and he curls up tightly and puts his head on my chest. He drinks the hot chocolate I have brought him.

"Anya," he says half-asleep. "Anya." *Mother.*

He is holding a soft toy from the nursery, the octopus he loves so much and he won't let go. I try to prise it out of his fingers but he grips tighter. Maybe he needs more than two arms to hold him and the octopus gives him that. I feel like he is my son. We can't even do anything physical so we just fall asleep. When I wake up at 6am he is still holding the plush toy octopus, its soft tentacles wrapped around him, the childish smile grinning at me. István is sleeping heavily, sighing and squeezing the toy. I am relieved when this happens and he is not having nightmares and I stroke the curls from his forehead with my hand gently so I don't wake him up.

My darling, how did I find you? How did my soul lead me to you in southern Hungary?

It is going to take about another 1000 years of seeing the shrink to sort this out.

One evening I am in a restaurant waiting for István to come back from the bathroom. Two women older than me are looking over. One comes to my table and addresses me in Hungarian.

"You're married to István, that dentist aren't you? You poor girl. No one has been with him very long, he hates women." She looks at me. I don't need this bitch's wasted pity. I love him like nothing on earth.

"You're just jealous. Why don't you go and find someone on your level, like here."

I put my hand to the floor. "You ugly old tarts."

I finish by chucking my glass of water over her just as István is coming back from the counter.

He might be half-crazy but he is my man. And I am half-crazy but I am his. A good match, you might say.

This woman looks at me and although she wants to slap me she sees the look in my eyes; the look of a Sicilian woman who would drag her to the floor and kick her.

István's presence and his look of disgust at her, not of me makes the two bitches leave fast.

"I would have smacked you, if you weren't pregnant, you bitch," one shouts as they exit.

For the first time I've known him, he laughs and laughs.

"Her sister went out with me years ago. She lasted all of a week. You're a real Italian firecracker, aren't you?"

I tell him, *I defend my man to the death. After all he is the most handsome man I have ever seen.*

"They don't have the most handsome man in the world forever but I do," I tell him.

He looks at me anew, with such pride. "Well you are," I say. "A bit strange, but then I like that too."

He tickles me and is playful. This is the first time we are shed of the obsessive love and jealousy, even just for the night. We lie in bed and laugh; we know it isn't really us, this is just the eye of the storm, but it feels good.

However, I can feel the slide into winter and I haven't got my safety net. It is October and I am afraid. I wake up a lot in the night afraid I have turned into a fat person and István isn't there. I get up worrying he has had a heart attack and is lying on the bathroom floor dead, although he has been checked and the time he thought it was his heart, it was anxiety and they gave him valium.

Which he refused to take. It is in the bathroom cabinet. And I would kill for a valium right now. A big fat pill to stop me feeling. Or more like two or three.

Where I find him these nights is sitting in the nursery playing with the toys. He doesn't look sad or happy or anything; no emotions are there. He is sitting on the floor with the soft toys speaking to them tenderly in Hungarian. I don't let him know I have seen him but I am disturbed by the blank look he has on his face, as if his soul has left his body. His favourite toy is the plush octopus and he is always clutching it as he sits on the floor or brings it to bed. He hides it under our bed until he thinks I am asleep then gets it out. I know, I just don't want to say anything as it is in complete contrast to his animal passion and then when I feign sleep, he pulls out his soft toy. When he is sitting in the nursery in the middle of the night I don't know if he is sleepwalking or just in a trance.

I just hope he is rehearsing for Natalija and not losing his mind.

Because I know it might only be a matter of time before I lose mine.

KARÁCSONY

It's snowing, it's late November and I can't believe I am pill-free. Apart from the awful Paris trip and some other moments we haven't had the volcanic eruptions of the past. He is leaving my passport in the apartment instead of jealously guarding it as though his prize will be stolen by someone else. It doesn't feel like flat-lining but I feel strange in this alien existence. This handsome husband who comes home happy to see me every day. After so long living on edge, swinging up and down between two poles of existence, it is hard to live in happiness as I am so afraid of losing it. But there's one thing I haven't done. I have bought new clothes, I have put the tiny dresses away. But I still haven't looked at myself naked in the mirror. I always wear a bathrobe. I shower with the lights out. I get into bed before I take my robe off as I am afraid of István feeling disgusted. I don't tell him this. He doesn't act disgusted but if I give it a voice I am afraid of putting the idea in his head.

I am afraid. *I want to throw up. I want to make myself thin again.*

My caesarean section is scheduled in for 1st December. I have to keep looking in the mirror naked now to remind myself the weight I feel I am walking around with is not fat but pregnancy as my mind is playing tricks on me. This is the first unravelling I am feeling. I am stripping off as many as 20 times a day to check I'm not fat as I have gained another 4 kilos. The day before I go into hospital I am 14 kilos heavier than the beginning of April. This horrifies me. My stomach is pushed out and hard to touch, the skin stretching unnaturally. There is nothing beautiful about it. When I feel her against my insides I do not feel joy like I should, I do not feel happiness but fear. My doctor does not understand me. He tells me after my first baby, I will want more pretty soon. I am such a beautiful girl I will have lovely children with my handsome husband who must surely want a boy as well as a girl. Don't I want to give him a son? I tell him *he has no fucking idea. I have enough trouble with one. And I am not having any more. One is enough.*

I want to hit the doctor every time I see him. I want to punch his lights out.

And he does not understand István who longs for a daughter in a way he would never if it was a son, although he would be happy enough he has said before. Happy enough whatever as long as she or he is beautiful. Beauty to him is everything.

But he is longing for his daughter in a way he never longs for anything.

I have an overwhelming desire to make myself throw up after every meal. I have to fight it and sit on my hands, do anything to stop myself. In the evenings it's okay as István is there but in the day I am afraid I will give in to the urge. I'm all baby, no Kiára. This makes me so mad. I am hating Natalija right now. I can already see her with her jet black hair and dark eyes demanding more of me every day while István comes home after work and sees his beautiful princess. *Only it is not me this time.*

It is the first winter in my life where I am not already depressed, but I am afraid of the darkness which is moving slowly in the distance like a horrible tornado in one of my recurrent nightmares as I can see the sickness is going to return. I am living on borrowed time. I don't want to talk about it in case I make it real. The feelings I am having for Natalija are not maternal and I am afraid this makes me sick. I see her as a threat, another woman in István's life. I don't want to hate her but I already do. Maybe I should just leave them both even though this is what I longed for so long. *I am going crazy.*

István is an orphan. His parents died in a car crash in Austria when he was twenty and at medical school. He doesn't say, but I know he is obsessed with car crashes. I have caught him watching car crashes on a loop he keeps in a locked box. He is terrified that this makes him strange to me but I am relieved he is not watching old girlfriends and porn. He doesn't need to tell me, I know from before. He is also an only child and it's only in the last few months he has been able to talk about it to me, the loneliness, the closing everyone out in case they left him, the work which became the focus of his life from the moment his parents died and he just lost himself.

He tells me, *he is afraid of losing me too, has always been afraid I would disappear and he would never see me again. It was only when he felt he could anchor me in some way the relief was immense. The darkness which haunted him now and then lifted only slightly when he married me.*

He thought, *Finally she is mine forever. No one else can have her.*

There is passion when he says this. I love his possessiveness. I love the fact he has admitted to it; the raging jealousy.

He says, *he was afraid I would still run away before then and take his child to another man and he would never find me.*

He doesn't say it but he is still afraid of me leaving.

Neither of us says it.

"I would kill myself," he says so suddenly.

"Hey," I say. "Don't say that, don't think that would have ever happen."

He is silent and looking at the floor. "Come here," I tell him pulling him into my arms. "It's okay now". He surrenders to being held.

"Promise you will never leave me," he says. "Please never leave me. I'd die. My heart would just break"

"As if I ever could," I say stroking his face.

He is a child at times like this. He needs his mother, I think. His parents' death is not something he wants to talk about but they were nice and loving as far as I know. They gave him everything and he shut down after they died, unable to even visit their graves in Debrecen, unable to face it. I think of him bottling his pain for all those years, burying himself in work, afraid to be close to anyone in case they left him. Despite all that he has with his profession and money and his looks and all the charm he can come up with when he is feeling good, he has no close friends or family, only acquaintances and distant relatives.

He closed everyone out and trapped me inside. I make up my mind I have to take him to Debrecen in May which is the anniversary of their deaths. He has to visit them in the cemetery.

I have my own demons and they are growing. In the darkness at night I need sex to feel beautiful. I need so much of it that István is telling me to stop. I ordered a load of porn magazines and lingerie which shocks him when he unearths them in the closet. He is very reserved in some ways and these magazines freak him out. His gentle and protective nature is annoying me and I almost want the angry, jealous rough man he can become in the bedroom but he's obsessed that it will harm the baby now and this makes me mad, like I have become all baby and no Kiára. Just carrying his child and nothing else. "There is nothing of me left," I scream. "I only have a week and they cut her out of me, just be rough, do what you have to do." The shrink sessions since September have had an effect on him and he is just gentle all the time. He has bought more toys for the nursery for Christmas and is disappointed when I am not sharing in his delight. He is so excited thinking of his new little girl whereas I feel nothing.

I am messed up and I tell him I have been thin all my life, I feel fat and it scares me so much, I have to do something to feel beautiful.

"You are beautiful. You are always beautiful," he tells me. "You were beautiful when I met you, you are beautiful now. When you got too thin, you were less beautiful because you looked ill. Now you are healthy, please be happy, darling?"

I lie on my side and Natalija is restless, stopping me sleeping. I am getting sick, I can feel it. I need her out of me so I can feel light, like I am me again not hauling this weight around that makes getting out of the goddamn car or up from the sofa difficult. It has made me feel so afraid and she is stretching my skin as if it will burst. I will explode like ripe fruit if she grows any more in this week. I wake up those last few nights screaming "Stop it, leave me alone, please stop," as she kicks me and balls her fists into my insides. I am soaked in sweat and tears and István is putting on the light, for once I am the one having the nightmares and he is the comforter. I tell him I can't remember the dream. *I can't tell him the truth. I can't tell him I hate my daughter.*

BÖRTÖN

The sky is eternity white
The trees are stencilled
Stark black
Ebony
The word bleak doesn't begin to describe

I feel
Nothing

It escalates with the hospital. That's when I start to feel everything sliding away. It is 1ˢᵗ December and I am not afraid of surgery, not afraid of the c-section. István is with me. He holds my hand as I have the surgery although I say I am fine and then he holds Natalija as they seal the wound and that's when I feel the old greyness coming back. She is heavy; 4.7 kilos but healthy. It's when I see István overcome with emotion and holding her while I feel nothing. Nothing at all. I should feel better now my body is mine again. I should feel happy to see her healthy.

I should.

"She is so beautiful," he says to me or to anyone or himself. I really don't care. "My little girl," he says kissing Natalija's face. He cradles her as though he waited his whole life for this moment and tears drip through his closed eyelashes. *I turn away. I am no longer needed.*

I don't want to look at her. I am almost glad of the excuse of the operation so I don't have to hold her. I can't make myself smile. I don't want her near me; I don't even want to touch her. I just close my eyes. I hear István say "Please look at her, Kiára, please just open your eyes and look at our little girl. She is so perfect."

I can't. I don't answer him. I pretend I am asleep.

When she is in her crib next to our bed I am kept awake at night. Not by her. I couldn't have asked for a better behaved girl. She sleeps through the night. She cries very little but I am struggling. My c-section makes everything difficult but I think I am going a little crazy. The first night out of hospital I am putting on my sexy lingerie and demanding sex from István who is too afraid of hurting me. He doesn't want to burst my stitches, he keeps telling me they need to heal. I can hardly stand up without my stomach hurting and I am pulling on stockings and fuck-me shoes. I need to be taking my medicine but I feel like I can't yet as I am admitting to something I don't want to admit to.

I have to feel sexy again. I got them to fit an IUD while I was in the operating theatre as I don't plan on more kids. One is enough and there is no way I am having any more accidents, since István doesn't take any responsibility in this department. He isn't the one who has to go through it all, after all. He just ends up with a perfect kid to complete what he sees as his perfect life and then he can go to work and leave me with it all day. No doubt he wants more kids in the future as he has always used the plural 'children' but he is not winning over that. I am sure over this one and he will thank me for it when Natalija starts walking and talking and demanding things and waking us up or God forbid, rattling the door when he wants sex. I can't see him dealing well with that.

In the middle of the night in his half sleep, I trick him into sex but there's no denying my stitches are hurting, my insides are screaming all through and I am crying afterwards. I am in so much pain I think I'm going to die. He is so upset, saying he feels like a monster. It's only been five days since my c-section and he's hurt me. I'm bleeding, the scar is weeping pus and he's trying to comfort me and clean me up. I am hysterical saying, *Natalija has ruined me, my body is ruined.*

He is telling me, *I am just healing, it will all be okay in a month or two when I am back in shape.*

I think, *So I am out of shape, this is what he is saying. I am fat, ugly, damaged, my skin still not back in place but sagging and swollen around the scar as if I will never be thin again. Damn her.*

He has to restrain me each night I am demanding him to fuck me. I am crazy as he holds my wrists as I slap him and pull his hair.

He says, *please stop hurting yourself, your body is not healed and you are treating me like I'm just an animal. I don't want to hurt you again. I want to care for you.*

I have to feel beautiful and when he refuses I get mad and accuse him of not finding me attractive any more. I can see he is doing it for my own good.

He's dying for me, he says, *but after the other night we are not doing anything until my body is healed. He can't kiss me as he wants to fuck if he kisses.*

The most I get is being held tight. I am getting into bed with stockings and high heels and red lingerie and this weeping scar which isn't healing. It's the first time he gets impatient for a long time and says he expected to be kept awake by Natalija and not by a sex-crazed wife.

He tells me, *to stop, stop hurting me and stop hurting him.* He holds me and stops me moving my arms below his chest. He doesn't want to lose control.

I am the one crying into the night, quietly. I don't want to make him angry.

My c-section is infected and I have to take antibiotics. It is hardly surprising given I am not eating. I ate healthily until I had Natalija and now I don't need to, I figure. I want to feel my bones through my skin again. And I am never hungry. István is back to working his 12 hour days and I am left alone with the winter and Natalija. He hires a housekeeper and au pair to help me as I am still unable to do much. I am paranoid. *He is avoiding me*, I think. He is tired when he comes home so I don't tell him my fears, I don't tell him the depression is coming back with a vengeance. I can see it now, the evil tornado in the distance. I can feel the wind whipping up and I am afraid. I can hardly go near Natalija as I am afraid I will break her, she is fragile. I can't lift her anyway, due to my stitches. I can't even lift the kettle full of water. I am hopeless. I am a washed up, burnt out mess.

Christmas is a blur. The only consolation is I am not alone. István takes ten days away from work. He is happy and healthy. I am sickly and depressed, hiding the uneaten food from my plate under the ornaments when he turns to look at Natalija. He is softer, glowing and calm. He seems to have shed his cruel sadistic side or maybe it is just waiting to emerge again. Either way, it is not me who brought this change in him but this little girl who does nothing but sleep. He is unwrapping toy after toy for Natalija who is too young to care and he is giving me gifts I don't want or need. I have tried to make an effort, making some dinner, buying him presents he is happy with, trying to smile when I want to cry. It is fooling him but I am not fooling myself.

But he notices. He asks me in bed when it is dark and he knows I won't lie. "Please tell me, Kiára. Please tell me if you are not well. You are not the same and I am worried about you. You only want sex but you are distant, please tell me if you need help."

I tell him, *I am okay* and start to kiss him to keep him quiet. I can't stir the monster that is waking up in my head.

He moves his head away saying *he can't touch me too much,* telling me *not to kiss him it is making him crazy with desire and it will hurt me.*

Let me just hold you, he says.

"You've changed Dr Sex Mad," I say nastily and turn over.

"Kiára," he says pulling me towards him. "I know you are not well. Let me get you some help, please tell me what is going on."

But I don't and I fall asleep as he holds me tight. I should be happy he is being so tender, I should be happy he is not cruel but nothing is touching me in my prison.

One week he attends a conference in Italy. I lose the plot. It's the middle of January and my body has healed but my mind hasn't. I am convinced he has gone there to fuck as he won't touch me sexually until I am completely healed. I get a knife out of the drawer in the kitchen and start my long-gone ritual in the bathroom complete with candles. Natalija is asleep. I think if she had been a screamer I would be dead by now. Sleepless nights would have driven me over the edge. Lucky for István too given his need for sleep and his own nightmares which he still won't talk about. Ironically, he is the one to wake me in the middle of the night screaming, not the baby. She hardly stirs when he is wrestling with his nightmares and I have to calm him. He is shouting out loud and little Natalija just sighs and turns over. I can't hate her however much I did before I saw her. I love her but I don't know what to do with her. I feed her and talk to her and change her and tell her my worst fears, that I am losing my mind. Maybe I shouldn't be telling her my darkest secrets but I can't trust anyone else. She doesn't know what I am saying, she just hears my voice and reaches for my hair, twisting it in her hands and settles against me to sleep while my tears drip down my face and onto her body. I spend a long time staring out of the window at the snow, hating southern Hungary. I begin to wish I was in Budapest with the life of the city outside my window. Here in the winter there is nothing. I am hating everything I once liked.

When István returns with a box of Italian chocolates and his beautiful smile, I am happy. I pretend the week was fine, fine. He's called me every evening to check I'm okay. He's sent his friends over in the five days he's been away and they have found me fine, fine. He rushes past me to see Natalija and I am fighting the dragon in my head which is screaming, *He only wanted her, not you.*

I forget what I've done with the kitchen knives and myself. I am doing my ritual of sexy lingerie and fuck-me shoes and silk dressing gown while I set his dinner place and that's when he notices. I'm acting weird, like I'm a bit high. I'm feeling a bit manic and I've been cooking Chinese. I throw the whole packet of fortune cookies in the air asking him to choose a coloured wrapper and this is when he sees that I've cut lines into my arm with the kitchen knife. They are crusted with jewels of blood. He sees this as the dressing gown falls loose.

"What have you done, baby? What the fuck have you done?"

He pulls my sleeve up while I am shouting and trying to wrestle my way loose. The dinner is getting cold.

"The crispy seaweed, István," I say. "It won't wait." I laugh hysterically at this and then I want to cry as he unravels the full damage. I can't look at him.

The slashes on my arm go all the way to the top. He always asked me what I'd done before and I would lie and say I was very accident-prone but this is not before. This is now and it's all too real.

"How can you do this to me?" he says. "I thought you were over self-harming, how can I leave you alone when you do this to yourself? How can I leave you alone with Natalija?"

I'm crying. "I'm sorry, please forgive me, I couldn't stop. I would never hurt her, I promise you."

He goes and sits in the living room his head in his hands. I follow him and try to hold him. He gently but firmly pushes me away.

"Please hold me, István," I say. "Please forgive me."

"Leave me alone," he says quietly. I go to the doorway. He is crying with his head in his hands on the sofa. I want to comfort him but I know he will push me away. He's a man who never cried and now we're crying all the time, both of us.

Fuck the crispy duck. I made it only for him given I am vegetarian after witnessing a train suicide. It makes me sick to cook meat and here it is in all its fleshy glory and he doesn't even want it. The plates are still in the dining room. Green tea in cups and fortune cookies.

Fortune cookies; that is a joke. I take a mouthful of seaweed and I take a cup of green tea into the bedroom, check on Natalija. She's lost in her angelic sleep. I look at her and I pray she won't turn out like me and swallow two valium and go to bed. I am drifting away and István is climbing in next to me sighing. I touch his black curls and his face. He moves away from me as far as he can to the other side of the bed.

I cry silently until the valium kicks in and I pass out. *He doesn't want you*, the voices in my head say, stretching through my nightmares like bubble gum.

I wake up in some grey hour, that dead winter hour between night and morning and the salt from his tears is in my mouth and on my face and he says, "I want you, baby, since I first saw you, I wanted you as mine. Don't ever leave me," he says in my ear but it sounds aggressive. He pulls my hair too hard.

What have we become? Where is the sweetness I tasted before?

He takes my arm, the cut one in the funereal morning light and kisses it, he licks the wounds as he is crying and telling me he's sorry. He's failed me. And I say *no, it's me. I failed you.* We are wrapped up in each other, all limbs and tongues and my head is a mess. I kiss him like the last time on earth and taste my blood. It feels like the first time but also the last time, the end of the world.

I feel that if we get out of this bed, we'll be separated forever.

It's all sliding away from me, faster and faster.

I'm not allowed to be alone after this. He has taken the sharp knives away and says he will get take outs from restaurants and I am paranoid it's because he thinks I will hurt Natalija, something that I would never do, if anything I am afraid of her. She is like a china doll I am afraid to touch. I don't believe she came from me, this thought is so real that if I didn't have my scar on my stomach I would actually believe it. I can't tell anyone this. The nurse comes to visit me and asks me how I am getting on and I am acting all the time for people. Smiling, making them a coffee, saying everything is just great. I can't even say one word I am feeling as I am afraid I will break down and they will take me away to some grim psychiatric ward. I am afraid they'll get rid of me and István will find someone new, who isn't so fucked up. I don't see that he is so worried about me right now, he wants to keep me safe; that he never thought I would hurt Natalija in a million years.

He knew I would only hurt myself.

It's March when he thinks he can leave me for a week while he goes to America for a course. It is soon after his birthday and I have tried my best and made him a cake, bought him gifts and feigned happiness so he feels wanted and loved. But I know I am not going to last a week without him at this stage. It is still winter and the sky is beaten lead.

This is serious. He doesn't know but he senses as I turn away and he holds me and says, *he doesn't want to go to America, he is afraid for me.*

I am afraid for me but I don't want him to resent me for stopping him. He wants to cancel it as he thinks it might be too early for me but I say I am fine. He is looking forward to this course. I tell him I will be okay really.

I smile, "Go! I know you will be happy to go and it isn't long, just a week."

I am lying. Every hour feels like a million years right now. When he is in work, the cruel clock in the kitchen cuts up the minutes into moments of pain. Pain to be in my head, pain to be awake and not asleep. And I want to cut. I want to cut my body to stop the pain but I can't as István's pain afterwards is too much. I can't hurt him like that again. And right now, a week feels like eternity.

His dark depthless eyes tell me he doesn't believe me, he is not sure I am okay, I am very fragile. He promises there will be people coming to see me all the time to help and he seems to think I am much better. I just need some help with Natalija and the housework.

In fact I am worse than ever. I haven't been taking medication apart from a rare valium as I don't want to pass it to Natalija in my milk. *I need to be on my medication again and give her a bottle but I am afraid it will stop me being close to her as this is the only chance I have to hold her and talk to her. I am ashamed of hating her when I first saw her; I am a bad person. I should really tell someone, anyone.*

SÖTÉTSÉG

I am not another Hungarian suicide statistic although there are so many. But I am selfish. I almost left István and Natalija when she was only four months' old. I thought I had the depression under control since I was off my meds. I thought finally I had the life I longed for but it was so fleeting, that moment; sunny skies whisked into a thunderstorm and light into darkness. Then creeping in, like smoke under the door little by little the old ghosts came back to haunt me; *You're horrible, you're ugly, you are useless, you are a worthless bitch. He doesn't love you and you're a lousy wife and mother. And yes, he is with someone else in America. You deserve to die, Kiára.*

Until their voices filled the smoke-choked room with a deafening refrain and I couldn't hear anything else. I couldn't hear István when he called me every day from America. I pretended it was a bad line because I could only hear the voices in my head and not what he was asking me, which was, *Are you okay? Darling, you are so quiet. Is there something wrong?*

And the images in my head were of someone with him, someone holding his hand as he spoke to me on his cell phone. Someone blonde and beautiful lying across his hotel room bed and him smiling at her, whilst all the time he talked to me. I could almost touch the image it was so real. It was more real than anything in the room I was actually in.

After this, I saw no reason to live. I could only see this image burned across my brain. I could even hear him telling her "My wife doesn't understand me."

I could only visualise him fucking her.

I just had to put a stop to these thoughts and they

would never stop unless I died. My head and heart feel as though they are full of needles and the pain is so sharp I can hardly breathe.

He and Natalija would be better off without me. So would everyone but especially István. He can have a more beautiful queen, a beautiful American blonde. I will be brave and disappear but not into the labyrinth of Spain. This time it has to be final. Make no mistake, Kiára. You deserve to die. You must die and leave him to the woman of his dreams.

I didn't talk about it. I fought the demons alone or tried and failed, afraid to talk about them in case he left, in case I had to go to hospital, in case people thought I was crazy. I thought I would lose him but I was wrong. I should have talked, I should have realised the depression would come back. He would have understood, people could have helped me. I realise that now.

In the end, he was the one who nearly lost me.

I did what I did because I listened to the voices in my head. I did what others had done years before me. I asked the au pair to look after Natalija for a bit longer that Tuesday, I left a note for Katalin to tell her, *please not to contact István in America. He will be home in 3 day*s. I ask her, *please forgive me.*

I drove to Budapest, leaving the car somewhere I can't even remember and I walked up the Szabadság Híd, climbing up the green sloping iron to the top.

'Please don't, please talk to me, I know what you're going through. Please come back if only for five minutes and talk to me. I won't make you stay. You are not a prisoner.'

My guardian angel. I am clinging to the top of the Szabadság Híd. The voice seems to come from heaven and it's dark but I don't know if it's night or just night in my head.

My hands won't let go. I am clinging to the top, unable to jump. Then I think of István with this other woman who has become so real to me and I let go of the iron and plunge to my death into the dark water.

I realise later when I am in what I think is Heaven that the voice was an older Hungarian man who was walking past and saw me scrambling up in high heels, a white wedding dress and tear-stained face. He said he thought I was a bride who had been jilted at the altar.

I was taken to Szent János Kórház. I don't remember much as they drugged me, I was talking rubbish and they were giving me shots of something and it made me sleep. István's face floats in front of me, beautiful and heart-broken in my dreams and he is screaming my name and the hospital doctors are restraining him and he keeps screaming "Kiára, Kiára!" and I want to shout to the doctors to *help him, please help him to get to me. Please let him hold me one last time. He told me he would die without me, what have I done?*

I realise I have died and left him. I am begging for forgiveness. I am begging forgiveness from God for leaving my little girl although I had forsaken God a long time ago. *Please take me back to earth, please take me back to them.* I am crying. I don't know if I have gone to Heaven or Hell as everything is merging faster and faster. I am crying for Natalija, the little girl I will never get to see grow up, for being so selfish as to leave her when she is helpless.

I will do anything to go back to earth, please give me forgiveness, please.

I am back in Spain in the cathedrals kneeling before Jesus on his crucifix for as long as it hurts, praying for help and forgiveness. I am climbing the Calvari steps with a giant crucifix in Mallorca, each of the 365 steps to atone for the sins of the past year. *God forgive me just give me one more year with them.*

I am awake when I am in my apartment or dream of my apartment as I think I am dead at this point. I am shouting for one more year and István comes running in. I am touching him and he feels real and asking him *are we in Heaven, is he really there or am I in my dream and where is Natalija? Where is the woman he was with?* The tears are on his face and I feel them on my hands and he tells me he will fetch Natalija now. Katalin did call him in America, the hospital in Budapest called him in America as they searched my bag and found out who I was. They told him I had been pulled out of the Duna river. I am telling him I could see him with a woman in America, I thought he had gone to someone else but even as I say it and I see his hurt eyes, I know it's not true. He tells me *he could never even touch another woman, even if I was dead.*

"God forbid, Kiára, you are my only one forever. I would never be able to even think about it." He cries at the thought of my insecurity and pain. There are so many flowers in the room I could be at my own funeral as I lie stiff and still in the bed while I watch him wipe his tears away and I can't move. I am still confused as to whether I am alive or dead.

I was diagnosed with severe postnatal depression. He thought he had lost me. His flight back to Hungary was hell as he didn't know if I was still alive. He tells me the first call from the hospital made his heart feel like it was ripped out of his chest, there was some confusion when they were telling him I had climbed up the bridge and had thrown myself into the

Duna river as they were not sure if I would pull through as I had already had two heart attacks. I don't even remember whether I did or not but I did jump. They had to restart my heart as in the ambulance; I died twice. I was rescued from the river quickly, but my heart had been shocked with the fall and the plunge into the water. He didn't know how sick I was. I didn't tell him. I didn't know how sick I was until he tells me all this. I thought I was being logical and rational and that I had to die because he would have a better life with someone else and Natalija would have a better mother.

I have lost track of time and he tells me it is the end of March and I have been back in the apartment for 3 days after 2 weeks in hospital. There are bottles and bottles next to the bed he has just brought in to give me my evening dose. Anti-depressants, mood stabilisers, benzos plus some pills for my heart to make sure it doesn't go into cardiac arrest again as it has been damaged by my heart attacks after the fall; this is new for me but I am right back where I started only at super maximum dose. I am so drugged my speech is slurry. István goes to say goodbye to the au pair and he takes the pills with him just for those few minutes. He tells me later, *the hospital has ordered him not to take any chances. There is not even a butter knife in the kitchen.*

I don't know what they think I could do as I am nearly asleep again in just those few minutes he is gone. He brings in Natalija to see me and I am horrified of what I could have done; leaving this little girl alone, leaving István. She is awake, dark eyes full of innocence. I manage to hold her a little before sleep takes over. I think this is the first time I really have held her without me crying over her in her short lifetime but it is nice, her warm body next to me.

István gives her a bottle as I drift away and my hands drop like a rag doll; my body is so full of poison now.

I promised never to leave him and I nearly left both of them. I feel guilty as Hell. I am a bad person.

When I wake up again István is still sitting there on the bed watching over me. He knows I was very sick. I have told him it is not my first suicide attempt, I tried in Spain in the time he knew me and I never told him in case he thought I was crazy. I have also been hospitalised before but no one ever knew apart from my shrink. I took three days off work and said I had kidney problems. I covered up so well in my lifetime. No more lies and veils needed. I am broken with pretending.

"We are all crazy, baby," he says. "All of us. There are things I want to tell you but I can't. I will, but not now."

I know, I know.

He tells me he is only going to work mornings for a long time from now on, no more endless days. Just 7am until 2pm Monday to Saturday. He is never leaving me alone apart from this and while he is working, he will have people here all the time. I am not to be alone in the apartment. He tells me he envies my sleep on these pills. He has nightmares almost every night and has done for a long time. This time I don't wake up and hold him. I am dead for the whole night on these meds. But he can hold me when he wakes from his dreams and it helps.

I know, I think. *He was always shouting, clinging on to me, sleeping with the light on. I don't know if he is doing it less now because he is taking some sleeping meds too or just because I am too drugged up myself to notice. You will tell me when you're ready. Whatever darkness is there, hidden in the past, you can tell me.*

He looks at his hands and says "I will tell you one day. Not now. Right now we need to take care of you and Natalija."

I nod. He knew what I was thinking. He pulls a couple of bottles out of his pocket. He can't look at me when he says shakily they are for him. The doctor said he should take them to even out his moods and to help him to sleep without waking up in terror all the time and he wants to give it a go.

Just a small dose. He wants to try as he knows he will not get better by therapy alone. He knows he can't be in denial forever as whatever sickness he has, it is growing and we will not get better, either of us until we can face up to our demons together.

I am proud of him for admitting to it finally and I want to tell him but my tongue is thick and fuzzy I can only reach out and squeeze his hand. I also feel guilty as if I contributed towards this, this downfall. But I know he has always been like this and I am only the catalyst which whirled him into the tornado. He was only holding it off for so long, refusing to live, apart from work so he wouldn't feel anything or let anyone in. He is bipolar and neither of us needs to say it. He knows.

He leans across and strokes my face. His eyes are clear and lovely. I could still drown in those eyes but they are so sad now.

Thanks to me. I feel awful.

"I promised I would never leave you," I tell him. "And I nearly did. I died twice on the way to hospital. God forgive me. I did it because I thought you would leave me if you knew I was so sick and I thought you and Natalija were better off without me. Forgive me,

István, please forgive me."

I want to cry but the pills make it hard to feel anything. He holds me and tells me he would have died too if I died, if it weren't for Natalija he would have driven his car into a bridge. But he never would have left her alone. She would have been his reason to live.

This makes me feel worse. She should have been my reason to live too. And him.

"I am sick too," he says. "And it is not weak. We are not weak for being sick. I pray that Natalija doesn't inherit….." He can't finish the sentence. It is too much for him.

"Don't you worry now," he says. "I will make sure we are all okay."

I expected him to be angry with me but he says I need to stop writing *forgive me* all over the mirror in lipstick; I don't even remember doing this. He forgave me the minute he saw me but he doesn't know why I was wearing a white wedding dress. It's hanging by the closet.

I don't know, I tell him. *I wanted to be pure.*

I think back to the last time I wore a white wedding dress which was when I was a gothic teenager crying in cemeteries for no reason over gravestones of people I didn't know. I would wear the dress everywhere as I found it in a charity shop. My mother threw it away telling me I was behaving like a fruitcake, which sixteen year old wears a wedding dress to college for God's sake?

I see the beautiful ivory beads in the light and I have to put on the dress. Bought in Budapest before I jumped off the bridge. It seems like a long time ago, not a few weeks.

Let me put it on for you, you'll like it, I say. I try to

get out of bed and fall to the ground due to the pills. He scoops me up.

Later, he says gently, *later.*

No, no, I say, *please help me. I have to put on that dress.*

So he does and I lie on the bed in the crusted beads. *Antique frosting. I feel like a cake.*

I am having random thoughts. I try to remember what I liked before. It is hard to remember anything on these pills.

He smiles at me in the dress. *It is beautiful, you are beautiful. You look like a queen,* he tells me. *But really there is no need to......*

István, I say. *I am so sorry. I promise I will never ever.....*

It's okay, it's okay, he tells me. *You are my world. You are pure.*

EL DÍA DE LOS MUERTOS

And so I go back to the beginning. I go back to the start or to the end. If we forget where we came from, we will go back there. It is the law of inevitability. It is November but there is no chill in the still air, only the warmth of the sun in the cemetery overlooking Pécs. The sky is a beautiful deep blue or a cruel shade of mocking azure, whichever way you want to look at it; however your heart taints it and paints the world.

It is 1st November, Day of the Dead when I once danced in Mexico with orange flowers in my hair with the heat of the sun and the laughter of the people as they celebrate death and life as one, when the skin between the worlds is the thinnest. When the dead return to life just for one day to be with their loved ones.

He traces the outline on the stone with his soft, gentle fingers.

In Loving Memory
Kiára Árgenta
My love, my life, my everything

They couldn't restart her heart, he tells a woman who is placing flowers at a nearby grave. *It had already endured too much. She was getting better and then suddenly she had a cardiac arrest again a year later.*

"I'm sorry for your loss and your little girl," says the woman. "Really, I wish you all the best."

Then she leaves him to his sadness. I don't know why he has placed my maiden name on the stone and not my married name when he was so possessive. Maybe he knew I liked it so much. Maybe he knew I would always be his anyway. What does it matter now.

God did listen, he did give me one more year with them. But only that. The best year of my life.

Be careful what you wish for.

István sits for a while on the grass with Natalija. She is restless and wants to go home. She is too young to understand why they are there, why István is so heartbroken, why he is crying but I know she still wants to know where Kiára is, when she is coming home to play with her. She remembers me, but I don't know how long for. Maybe it is helped by all the photos he has placed in the apartment.

She must feel I abandoned her. She puts some of the orange flowers he has brought for the cemetery on her head like Day of the Dead in Mexico, like I did once when I was so carefree in the sunshine, before life got darker. Natalija gives him a beautiful smile and the orange looks so pretty on her black curls. It makes him smile too, just for a few seconds.

I am a traitor. I could never trust him totally because of my jagged heart. No wonder it failed me in the end. He didn't have the heart of thorns which closed everyone out; I did. It was too damaged to trust my love. It should be me taking care of him, not this tiny girl who is hardly old enough to speak but yet understands so much already. I promised him. I lied.

I will never rest. Hell doesn't exist; there are no flames, no gnashing of teeth and no screams of the sinners and the Damned. I am not burning forever more. The sweet mystic music has turned into a cacophony of shrill sounds, stretching into infinity. As I am in this place between the worlds of the living and the dead where I see and hear everything but no one can hear or see me, I am in my own Hell.

END

Kiára Árgenta

CHAPTERS and POEMS

	HUNGARIAN	ENGLISH
1	Jeges Pokol	Frozen Hell
	Temető	Cemetery
2	Égés őrültség	Burning madness
	Ajándékok	Gifts
3	Magyar lány	Hungarian girl
4	Vodka	Vodka
5	Szeret	Love
6	Tűz és Jég	Fire and Ice
7	Keresztre feszítés	Crucifixion
8	Hánytűz tél	Volcanic winter
	Utál	Hate
9	Norvégia	Norway
10	Sötét Város	Dark city
11	Remény	Hope
	Skorpió	Scorpion
12	Pók Háló	Spider web
13	Párizs őrültség	Paris madness
14	Smaragd- A szín	Emerald the colour of
15	Enyém vagy	Possession
16	Betegség	Sickness
17	Karácsony	Christmas
18	Börtön	Prison
19	Sötétség	Darkness
	SPANISH	ENGLISH
20	El Día de los Muertos	The Day of the Dead